MW01006901

A SHOT OF MURDER

A Charley Hall Mystery, Book I

Brenda Gayle

BOWSTRING
BOOKS

Bowstring
Books

A Shot of Murder
(A Charley Hall Mystery, Book 1)
by Brenda Gayle

Published Internationally by Bowstring Books
Ottawa, Ontario, Canada
Copyright © 2020 Brenda G Heald

All rights reserved. The use of any part of this publication reproduced, transmitted in any form or by any means, electronic, mechanical, photocopying, recording, or otherwise, without the prior written consent of the author, Brenda Gayle, is an infringement of the copyright law.

EBOOK ISBN 978-1-9990185-6-6
PRINT ISBN 978-1-7775824-1-8

This is a work of fiction. Names, characters, places and incidents are either the product of the author's imagination or are used fictitiously, and any resemblance to any person or persons, living or dead, events or locales is entirely coincidental.

For Madeline and Carolyn,
my two favourite Kingstonians.

"PLEASE SHUT THE DOOR, MRS. HALL."

Please? Missus?

Charley turned and pushed the door closed. John Sherman was the *Kingston Tribune*'s journalist-turned-editor. Hard-nosed and driven, he didn't take the time for niceties like using "Mister," "Miss" or "Missus"—never mind "please" and "thank you"—when he spoke to his reporters. The fact he chose to use both now didn't bode well. Charley took a deep breath, squared her shoulders and approached the desk.

"Sit!" Sherman ordered, not looking up from the copy he was reading.

"I'd prefer to stand." Charley wasn't prepared to abandon even the tiniest modicum of power. Sherman was a small man—only five-foot-four—and self-conscious about it. His own desk and chair sat on blocks, forcing unsuspecting visitors to look up at him when seated rather than look him square in the eye while standing. At five-foot-seven, Charley knew remaining standing was clearly to her advantage.

Sherman exhaled unhappily. "As you wish."

"Is that the piece I did on the prison guard murder?" A few hours earlier, prison guard and messenger John D.

Kennedy had been overpowered and killed by two convicts who'd then escaped the maximum-security penitentiary and were still at large. Charley had been having morning coffee with her grandmother when she'd heard the alarm being raised and rushed to the prison to investigate. An advantage of living in the shadow of Kingston Pen was that she was the first reporter on the scene, and she hoped to scoop her competition by getting her story in the *Kingston Tribune*'s early afternoon edition. "I thought I'd go to his home in Portsmouth and do a follow-up," she added. "Kennedy was an interesting fellow. His father worked at the Pen, and he was actually born in an apartment within the old west gate-house. And then, of course, there are the convicts them-selves. I was thinking—"

"Slow down, Hall!" Sherman stood and came around his desk. He paused, glanced up at Charley, and then circled back and resumed his seat. "There's something we need to discuss."

Charley's heart sank. Sherman wasn't the "discussing" kind of boss, either. Whatever was on his mind, she was certain she wasn't going to like it.

"You know, I've never been entirely comfortable having a woman—"

"Is there a problem with my work?" Charley cut in, anticipating where this was going. She'd been at the *Trib* for five-and-a-half years and he'd never shown any dissatisfac-tion with her reporting, but she wasn't blind to what was happening in the world.

He held up a hand to stop her. "Let me finish," he snapped. "I don't think women have a place in the news-room. I agreed to hire you in deference to your grand-mother—and out of respect for the memory of your grandfather, who founded this paper, and your father, of course, who was my friend and a terrific journalist in his own right."

"You gave me a job as a copy editor, editing other people's stories. I went out and proved myself as a reporter. I *earned* this job."

He nodded. "You're a good writer, I'll give you that." He glanced down at the typewritten pages in front of him. "And your instincts are good, too."

"Then why does it sound like you're firing me?"

Sherman's pale complexion turned pink. He took off his wire-rimmed spectacles and rubbed his bloodshot eyes. "Things were different back when you came looking for a position here. We were fighting a war. There were jobs but not enough men to fill them. That's changed. It's been over two years since we defeated Hitler and Tojo." He put his glasses back on and stared at her. "Our soldiers have returned home and need to support their families. Don't you think it's time women went back to taking care of their men and having children? That's how this country is going to recover."

Charley was all too aware of the toll the war had taken on its young men, but it wasn't fair to ask her and other women, who had made a real contribution in their absence, to resume their previous lives of domesticity. There had to be a way to forge a new society where men and women could work side-by-side. Her grandmother had been one of the women who'd fought for women's suffrage at the turn of the century. And it had been almost twenty years since women had been recognized as "persons" under the law with the same rights and privileges as men.

"I'm assuming you're coming to me now because you've found someone you want to hire," Charley said. "Look, I'm happy to share my workload with any new reporter you care to bring on. There's enough going on in Kingston to keep us both busy."

"The *Trib* can't afford both of you."

"So that's it? You're throwing me out into the street?"

Sherman's eyebrows raised quizzically, and Charley immediately regretted her outburst. So dramatic. So stereotypically female. Just the response he'd be looking for so he could justify his decision.

"Well, of course, I'm not speaking literally," she snapped. Sherman knew full well she lived with her grandmother in a lovely red-brick colonial home situated in one of the better areas of the city. "But what am I supposed to do? I have no husband to take care of." She saw Sherman blanch at that. Good. She wanted to make him uncomfortable. She wanted to remind him she wasn't immune to loss from the war. It was only when she was deep into a story for the *Trib* that the constant ache of Theo's absence was soothed. She pressed on with her argument. "I have no children. And my grandmother has a housekeeper, so I'm not needed for domestic chores."

"Well," he sat back in his chair looking altogether too pleased with himself, "if you insist on continuing here, I do have one opening."

Darn it. From the look on his face, he'd been leading her on, hoping she'd react as she had so he could force her to take a position she knew already she wasn't going to like.

"Mildred Preston is retiring—"

"No!" Charley stared at him, horrified. "I will not take over the women's pages." Going from reporting real news to writing fluff pieces about parties and clothes? She couldn't imagine it.

"It's better than copy editing, and you'd still be able to write."

4

"What will the readers think when they see Charley Hall's byline on an article about Dior's fit-and-flared look for Spring '48?"

Sherman snorted, amused. "Frankly, Hall, I'm impressed you're up on Dior and the latest fashion trends. You've just proven to me that you *are* the woman for the job. And as for the byline, of course it can't be Charley Hall. But it can be Charlotte Stormont."

Her maiden name.

"I won't do it."

"Don't decide right now. Mildred says she'll stay on until we have her replacement. Take a few days to think about it."

How could he do this to her? The women's pages? She didn't need a few days to think about it. She knew her decision right now. But Sherman didn't need to know that. "In the meantime, can I follow up on my story?"

"No. The new guy's starting today. I've assigned the Pen murder to him. But I will put your byline on the scoop. That was damn good reporting."

CHARLEY KICKED the door closed and dropped her red leather case on the marble tile of the foyer. The brisk, thirty-minute walk from the *Kingston Tribune*'s office on Bath Road to her home on King Street West did nothing to improve her mood. She was still bristling over Sherman demoting her. She'd worked hard to earn her spot.

It's not fair I'm out simply because I'm a woman.

"Gran?" she leaned against the banister to the stairs and called out. "Are you home?"

"Uhmph!"

Charley whirled around to see a young woman she didn't recognize struggling with the case she'd left by the door.

"What do you have in here, *Madame? Des roches?*"

"Who...?" Charley shook her head. "No, never mind. Here, I'll take it." She retrieved the case from the woman. "Not rocks. It's a portable typewriter." She put it down beside her feet and held out her hand. "I'm Charley, Mrs. Stormont's granddaughter."

"Bonjour, Madame Charley. I am Chantal, the new *domestique,* ah, domestic?" She shook her head in frustration. "What you call it?"

"Housekeeper." Charley eyed the young woman. She

7

couldn't be more than twenty—mousy brown hair, large blue eyes, and a mouth that seemed too big for her face. There wasn't much to her—she was just a slip of a thing. No wonder she'd struggled with the typewriter.

Gran hadn't mentioned she was hiring a new house-keeper, but Charley wasn't surprised to see Chantal. Her grandmother changed housekeepers almost as often as she changed her clothes. For some reason, they never managed to meet her criteria for service, and the one or two who were by some miracle up to snuff usually ended up quitting. Still, Charley had quite liked the last housekeeper. And the one before, too.

"Welcome, Chantal. I hope you'll be happy here."

"*Merci, Madame.* I certainly hope so." She curtsied awkwardly and then brushed past on her way to who-knows-where.

Charley had no idea how a household was run. Since her parents' deaths when she was a very young child, she and her brother had grown up amongst a succession of governesses and housekeepers. She wondered if Freddie had met Chantal yet. Two months at best, she decided. That would be her wager for this housekeeper. She wondered what her brother would bet. He tended to be more generous in his timelines—but then, he usually lost.

"Oh good, Charlotte, you're home."

Elizabeth Stormont, Bessie to her friends, descended the stairs, impeccably dressed as always, although her wardrobe hearkened back thirty or more years to her heyday as a society maven. Today she wore a pearl-coloured tea dress that flared slightly at her hips before descending to her ankles. Charley marveled at how she managed to keep her long, grey hair in a perfect brioche-shaped bun—not a strand escaping. She raised a self-conscious hand to her own shoulder-length, chestnut-coloured hair and tucked a wayward curl behind her ear.

"You won't believe what Sherman did today," Charley began.

"*Mister* Sherman, if you please."

"I doubt you'll be so deferential when you hear what he did," she said.

"I already know. He rang me up earlier and we discussed it. Come, I'll get the girl to brew up some tea for us."

Of course he did!

Charley gritted her teeth so she wouldn't say something she'd regret, grabbed her case and followed Bessie into the drawing room. Gran motioned for her to sit beside her on the couch, and then picked up a silver service bell and rang for Chantal.

Within seconds the new housekeeper ran into the room and curtsied. "*Oui, Madame.*"

"Some tea, please. Oh, and take Miss Charlotte's case up to her room."

"No, it's all right. I'll take it up when I go later," Charley said quickly, stifling a grin at the panic that had turned Chantal's eyes into large saucers. She turned to her grandmother. "I can't believe you aren't as outraged as I am about this."

"Well, what did you expect, dear? You know I wasn't happy about you traipsing all over town, *in trousers*, pretending to be a man. I think the women's pages will be a lovely change. You can wear dresses again, maybe do something a little more stylish with your hair." She reached out and tucked yet another unruly strand behind Charley's ear. "But that's not what I want to talk to you about."

"I am not pretending to be a man," Charley said,

9

refusing to allow her grandmother to change the subject. "And frankly, Gran, trousers are much more comfortable than dresses. You should try them some time. I think you'll be converted."

Gran wrinkled her nose at the suggestion. "Really, *Charley*? How many readers do you think know you're a woman? And do you think John Sherman would want his newspaper to have the reputation of hiring a woman to work on ugly stories like that terrible murder this morning?"

"First, I've been called 'Charley' all my life. Grandpa started it. You are the only one who insists on calling me 'Charlotte.' Second, it's not John Sherman's newspaper. He's simply the editor—an employee, like I am. And if anything, I have more right to be at the *Tribune* than anyone else there."

"Well, except perhaps for the man who purchased it from your grandfather," Gran said dryly. "And that man has put John, not you, in charge of its day-to-day operations." She paused as Chantal set the tea service on the table in front of her. "That's fine. You can go. I'll pour."

Charley watched the pale liquid trickle into the fine china teacup. She'd have preferred a black coffee—or something stronger—but this afternoon ritual seemed to mean a lot to her grandmother, and despite their differences, her grandmother meant the world to her. When Gran had taken her first sip, Charley went on the offensive. "You fought for a woman's right to vote. You marched in the streets. You were *arrested*. You taught me to be strong and independent. How can you not see the injustice in this?"

"You are not being fired from the paper. You are merely being reassigned to a position more suitable to your sex and social standing."

"I'm not going to take it. I don't want to get dressed up and go to all these hoity-toity social events—"

Gran had begun to giggle, quietly behind her teacup at first, but now her laughter shook her whole body and she had to put the cup down on the table or risk spilling its contents.

"What is so funny?"

"You." Bessie sobered. "As a Stormont, you already get dressed up and go to 'all these hoity-toity social events.' John is giving you the opportunity to do more than simply look pretty at them. You can write about who was there and who were the big contributors to whatever charitable cause was being celebrated. You will wield far more clout with the power brokers of Kingston on the women's pages than you ever could on the city ones."

"I don't want to do it," Charley said.

"Then don't." She shrugged and picked up her teacup. "There are many ways to be useful. The Imperial Order Daughters of the Empire is always looking for intelligent young women to join our ranks and aid in service to our country."

"I'll think about it." Charley took a last gulp of her tea and replaced the cup on the tray. "What was it you wanted to talk to me about?"

"Freddie's birthday is this weekend. I'd like to invite some of his old friends to a bit of a celebration. He seems to have withdrawn since he's come home. I thought a party might be just the thing to get him back to his old self."

She saw the worry in Gran's eyes and shared it. Freddie couldn't wait to sign up in 1939 when Canada followed Britain into the war against Hitler. But it hadn't turned out to be the adventure he'd expected. He had returned a different person, haunted by memories of battle and the

German POW camp that he wouldn't speak of. The demons he lived with seemed to quiet down only when he was lost inside a bottle. Gran didn't understand. Her husband and son had both been soldiers. Both wounded. Both returned, more or less whole. Why not her grandson?

Charley thought Freddie had been making progress. The second anniversary of his arrival back in Canada had been two weeks ago. She'd been on the lookout for the dark shadows that usually preceded a bender, but there had been none. Then, last Friday, he'd gone out and hadn't returned.

Three days was a long time to be gone, even for Freddie. Charley wasn't sure how much longer she could hide his absence from her grandmother. And now, with a party planned for the end of the week?

She stood and bent down to kiss Gran on the cheek. "I think that's a wonderful idea. I'll put a list together, shall I?"

CHARLEY PULLED the door closed and paused on the front step to her home to gaze up at the brilliant afternoon sunshine. After a slow start to spring, the last two days had been truly glorious, allowing her to shed her heavy woolen coat for a lightweight trench coat.

With Gran retiring to her room for a quiet afternoon of reading, Charley headed out in search of Freddie. She glanced to the east, wishing she could simply walk the ten minutes to the Queen's University campus to find her brother drinking with friends at one of the student pubs.

Bright, sensitive Freddie had been studying English literature for the sheer joy of it before the war broke out. Everyone had expected him to eventually take up a career as a reporter—everyone except Charley. She knew her brother was drawn to the esoteric nature of prose, not the cut-and-dried facts of journalism. Frederick Stormont I— Grandpa—probably knew, too, because he'd sold the *Tribune* when she and Freddie were still teenagers.

True, the stock market crash and subsequent economic depression had taken its toll on the family's finances—and Grandpa's health. Some thought his stroke had been brought on by the financial pressure he'd been under, but Charley couldn't help but wonder if the loss of his beloved newspaper had contributed to her grandfather's death. She was certain if Grandpa had had any faith Frederick Stormont III would follow in his footsteps—and those of his son's, their father—he'd have found a way to hang on to the *Trib*, and maybe survived.

If only Grandpa had considered me...

The sleek, red portable Smith-Corona typewriter she lugged back and forth to the *Tribune* had been a gift from their grandfather to Freddie on his thirteenth birthday. The exotic machine had sat in her brother's bedroom for years, eschewed by him in favour of longhand just as journalism was for literature.

By contrast, Charley's thirteenth birthday present had been a pair of pearl earrings, which were meant to signify her entry into proper female society.

Anytime he'd allow her into his room, Charley would explore the wonder of Freddie's typewriter. She loved everything about it, from the *clickity-clack* it made as the metal rods struck the paper once she got up speed to the *zip* of the carriage return lever as she began a new line of prose with barely a pause. But the best, the very best, was the feeling of the round metal keypads depressing so effortlessly beneath her fingertips to make physical the stories in her head.

Three years after he'd left to join the allies fighting in Europe, they received the awful news that Freddie was missing and presumed dead. Charley went to her brother's bedroom, packed up the Smith-Corona and moved it into her own room. Then she went to the offices of the *Kingston Tribune* and asked John Sherman for a job.

Even after her brother returned to them, broken by the war, she continued to carry the typewriter with her as a reminder there was a price to be paid for those easy keystrokes—a debt owing for her to continue the family legacy.

Charley shook off her melancholy, squared her shoulders and turned west to take the other ten-minute walk, past Kingston Penitentiary to the small village of Portsmouth.

Beaupre's Tavern—Beaup's as it was called by the locals —stood at the entrance to the harbour village and, given its proximity to the penitentiary, was a popular spot for many of the prison's staff.

As Charley entered the two-storey white building, she was surprised to see so many uniformed guards drinking in the main room of the tavern. It was common knowledge the Beaupre family, with many of its own members working at the prison, had a special room reserved in the back where men in uniform could drink freely, away from the prying eyes of prison officials. But today wasn't any ordinary day, and so she presumed the powers-that-be would overlook this violation of the rules.

She received more than her fair share of suspicious glances when she started asking about Freddie. However, once she'd satisfied them she wasn't an angry wife or a jealous girlfriend, they were much more forthcoming. A generous sprinkling of banknotes had helped to loosen their tongues, too.

Beaupre himself confirmed Freddie was a frequent patron, but he hadn't seen him for a couple of days. "But there was a woman…" one of the regulars had told her. So, armed with a likely address, Charley prepared to head deeper into the village, toward the shoreline and its seedier side.

But first, she'd take a small detour. She couldn't help herself. As anxious as she was to find her brother, she couldn't quite let go of the story—her story. She felt compelled to see the house where John Kennedy, the murdered prison guard, had lived. Ironically, his red wooden-siding home was on Kennedy Street, named after his grandfather, who'd been Portsmouth's reeve.

A small crowd had gathered to offer support to Kennedy's widow and son. She paused across the street to watch, itching to join them, to find out more about the unfortunate man—now proclaimed a hero—who'd been shot because he'd refused to hand over the keys to the North Gate.

She wondered what would become of Mrs. Kennedy. How would she get along now she was left to raise her son alone? Was there compensation for women whose husbands were killed in the line of duty as there had been for those killed in the war?

And what about the two convicts who'd escaped? Any news about them?

She hated being in the dark.

Two men stood slightly apart from the rest of the group, smoking cigarettes, laughing together, and scribbling on notepads. She recognized one as the crime reporter for the *Kingston Whig-Standard*, the competing newspaper. The other man was likely her replacement. She looked closer, noting the ill-fitted, baby-blue suit with the middle button on his jacket hanging on for dear life. He looked young and pallid—hardly the virile war hero she'd been expecting.

If he believed comparing notes with the competition was the best way to do his job, then he wasn't going to last long at the *Trib*. Newspapers lived and died by their scoops.

Buoyed with optimism for her continued employment, Charley set off to the address she'd been given.

The house, a square, two-storey, quarried limestone structure with yellow shutters and door, was much nicer than she'd expected given its location among the dilapidated old warehouses and tanneries. She knocked several times, but no one unanswered.

"Hello?" Charley peered through a crack in the blinds of one of the front windows, but she couldn't see anything in the dimness.

Frustrated, yet unwilling to give up, she circled around to the back of the house. There was a small garden plot. April was too early for planting, but someone had already started to prepare the soil in anticipation of warmer weather. Such a lovely spot, she thought, gazing up at the budding trees. It wouldn't be long before the air would hang heavy with the scent of lilac and flowering crabapple.

Enamoured with thoughts of spring, Charley almost missed the dried, rusty brown-coloured smudges on the wooden slats of the back porch. Someone, a woman judging by the shoeprints, had tracked something from inside the house to here, and then the marks abruptly stopped.

She must have removed her shoes... Charley bent down for a closer look.

"Oh!" She jumped back. *Blood?* She'd seen blood at crime scenes before. Usually, it was fresher, brighter, stickier. This was dried, sun-baked, but she was pretty sure it was blood.

She stepped around it and knocked on the back door before turning the handle and pushing it open.

"Hello? Anyone here? Freddie?"

The blood trail was thicker and still moist inside the house. She followed it past a collection of empty pots and gardening tools into the kitchen. The coppery smell she'd noted when she stepped across the threshold was much stronger here. A distinctive buzzing hum sent a shiver down her spine. *Flies.* She swallowed down the bile rising in her throat and allowed her eyes to adjust to the dimness of the interior.

Something's not right.

The room appeared untouched, pristine. Except there was blood everywhere. It was splattered against the walls, on the tabletop, across the cupboard doors. *And flies!* She turned to where the buzzing was coming from. Between the table and the icebox there was even more blood.

And a shape of something?

She took a step forward.

Someone—

"Dear God, no!"

CHARLEY RACED FORWARD, forgetting to be careful of the sticky mess on the floor.

No, no, no, no, no!

It couldn't be him. *Please don't let it be him.* She held her breath and steeled herself to look down at the unfortunate soul on the ground.

Relief so fierce, so visceral, it throbbed as it coursed through her. She stumbled backward and gripped the countertop for support.

Not Freddie.

She gave a fervent prayer of thanks and waited for the room to stop spinning.

When her legs finally felt able to bear her weight, she returned to the body, bending down to take a closer look.

It was a woman, a large woman, not heavy but tall with broad shoulders and a wide, square face. Her light brown hair was faded and streaked with silver. Likely in her mid-to-late fifties. There was a palm-sized bruise across her left cheek. Had she put up a fight? Charley leaned in. Not a bruise. Tiny striations of purple capillaries criss-crossing the woman's cheek. A birthmark? She didn't know whether to feel relief the woman hadn't been battered or sympathy that she'd had to bear the prominent mark her whole life.

The woman's brown eyes stared up at her. Unfocused. Dead. Charley resisted the urge to close them. She'd been to enough crime scenes to know the police became annoyed if anything was disturbed. Blood covered the woman's simple, belted, blue-and-white polka-dotted dress and had pooled beneath her. There was so much blood everywhere, but it seemed to emanate from a single source, up close to her collar bone.

Gunshot, if she had to guess.

Charley's mind immediately leapt to the escaped convicts. But no. That didn't make any sense. They had a car. And besides, there was only one small set of footprints leading away from the body.

She rose and glanced down at the floor and groaned. And now her own, considerably larger, footprints.

She had to call the police.

There must be a telephone somewhere.

Yes, she shouldn't disturb the crime scene, but it felt wrong to leave the woman alone. She slipped off her shoes and, doing her best to avoid stepping in any more of the blood, she headed toward the front of the house. Spying the telephone in the hallway, she made the call, and blew out a breath.

Padding back to the kitchen, she mentally kicked herself for forgetting her reporter's notebook. She scanned the room, trying to commit to memory the details of the scene.

The woman had been washing dishes when she'd been attacked. Charley put her finger into the water-filled basin. It was warm, so it couldn't have been too long ago. Rubber gloves sat neatly stacked next to the sink. She'd likely removed them to answer the door to the killer. Or, at least she'd had time to remove them before she'd been shot. Did that mean she'd known her attacker?

Tacked to the wall, beside the icebox, was a torn piece of newsprint with some droplets of blood. She looked closer, noting the *Tribune* masthead and four-month-old date. It must have been important for the woman to display it. But why had it been ripped down? And who had done it? The murderer?

"Mrs. Hall?" a gruff voice called out.

"I'm here. In the back. In the kitchen."

Charley was surprised she recognized the two Kingston Police constables who entered. "You fellas are a little out of your jurisdiction, aren't you?"

"We're simply helping out," Constable Marillo, the older of the two, said.

"You haven't touched anything, I hope," Constable Adams, the younger one—the one whose suggestion they meet for drinks she'd rebuffed a few weeks prior—said snarkily.

"I left my shoes by the body, so you can rule them out."

"Ease up, boyo. She knows the drill," Marillo said, stepping carefully toward the body. He picked up her brown stacked-heel oxfords, looked at their blood-stained soles, glanced at the two sets of shoe prints on the floor, then handed them back to Charley.

"So, I guess the regular Portsmouth crew are involved in the search for the escaped convicts," she said.

"Hmmm," Marillo grunted. "Do you know the victim?"

Darn, he wasn't giving anything away. "No," she said.

Adams sneered. "You often visit people you don't know?"

"I was following a lead," Charley countered smoothly. There was no way she was going to mention Freddie and his possible connection to the victim.

"Do you at least know her name?" Constable Marillo

asked, although she suspected he already anticipated her answer. Marillo had been a cop for a long time and still hadn't made detective. He wasn't a go-getter like Adams. He seemed content to do his work, train young officers, and then watch them pass him up the ranks without a backward glance or a thanks-for-your-trouble. She liked him, but she didn't understand him.

"Sorry, I don't know her name."

"Well, what do you know?" Adams snapped.

Now, someone like Adams she understood all too well, and she didn't like him one bit. He was arrogant, insensitive, and unfortunately destined for the higher echelons of the police force.

"I can't divulge my sources," Charley said while crossing her fingers behind her back. It was a childish affectation but it made her feel better about the deception. As she said the words, she realized she wouldn't be able to write about this murder for the *Tribune* as she'd first thought—at least not until she found Freddie. Not that she believed he had anything to do with the woman's death...

Oh, Freddie, where are you?

"I'm surprised you were able to get here so fast," Charley angled. Maybe she could get them to give her an update on the manhunt. "I thought everyone would be chasing the escaped convicts."

"We already got 'em," Adams boasted. "A couple of the prison guards found them cowering under some brush south of Sydenham after they ditched the car."

Bingo!

"Adams!" Marillo glared at his partner before turning to Charley. "That's not for publication. There'll be a formal announcement later, once we have a better idea about what happened. Understand?"

"Hey, not my story." Charley shrugged innocently. Boy, would she love to pursue *that* lead. A second scoop in one day. But Sherman had taken her off the beat, and besides, she had her hands full with trying to find Freddie.

"Just so we're clear: You're not to write anything about what you may or may not have heard from Constable Adams," Marillo repeated.

"Crystal." Charley smiled sweetly at Adams, enjoying his discomfort at being dressed down by his partner.

Marillo nodded, satisfied, and both men shifted their focus back to the dead woman on the floor.

"Wow. Take a gander at that bruise," Adam said. "She must have received quite the wallop from whoever did this."

"Or it could be totally unrelated," Marillo cautioned.

Charley started to correct them and then decided to let the constables figure it out for themselves. "Well, if you don't need anything else from me, I'll skedaddle," she said.

"Fine," Marillo said. "If we have questions, we'll be in touch."

"Don't skip town," Adams added unnecessarily.

Charley went out the back door, past the dried smudges of blood. She wiped the soles of her shoes clean on the grass before slipping them on.

What kind of jam have you gotten yourself in now, Freddie?

Frustration warred with irritation warred with genuine fear. She needed to find her brother, and not just because of Gran's birthday party plans.

She hailed a cab on King Street, anxious to get to the *Tribune*'s office and the one person she knew could help her.

CHARLEY IGNORED Sherman's questioning look as she raced through the newsroom and pushed open the door to the *Tribune*'s morgue.

"Well hello, Mrs. Hall," Grace Fletcher said, looking up from the ledger she was using to meticulously note the contents of the latest edition of the newspaper.

The "morgue" was the *Tribune*'s archives and Grace was the quintessential archivist. Younger than Charley, and with a university degree in library science—who knew such a thing existed?—Grace was a wiz at finding information. She looked the part, too: unimposing and nondescript with blondish hair, bluish eyes, and a wardrobe that blended in with her environment. Being in the background seemed to suit her just fine. And yet, Charley couldn't think of a major story she'd written in the last few years that hadn't been improved one-thousand-fold by Grace's research.

"I heard a nasty rumour you'd packed up your bright red Smith-Corona and left us," Grace said, tapping her pencil against her temple.

"Premature." Charley shrugged. "Nothing's been settled."

"And yet, there is a strange man sitting at your desk," she said, nodding toward the newsroom.

Charley glanced into the newsroom and noted the same fellow she'd seen in front of the Kennedy house was now sitting in her chair. She shrugged. "We'll see how long he lasts." She closed the door to the archives for privacy. "Grace, I need some help."

"Are you in trouble?"

"No, not me. It's..."

"Oh, for a story?"

Charley eyed her carefully, hoping Grace wasn't a mind reader, too. "Yes, of course, a story," Charley said, crossing her fingers behind her back. It was only a little lie. With any luck, it would turn into a story. First, though, she needed to find her brother and make sure he was safe.

She gave Grace a rundown of the murder she'd discovered and the torn newspaper clipping, omitting any mention of Freddie. It wasn't that she didn't trust Grace, but she didn't want to put her friend in a compromising position and jeopardize her job at the paper. Women were scarce at the *Trib* and she feared her own demotion may be just the beginning of the publication's new world order. "So, I need to know who the woman was and what article she had tacked up in her kitchen."

"If you give me her address, I'll see if she's listed in the city directory. In the meantime, you know where the old newspapers are stored. Have at it."

January 15, 1948. Page 1.

Thanks to Grace's exceptional organizational skills, Charley was able to retrieve a copy of the newspaper within minutes. It had been a Thursday. She opened the paper and laid it out on the work table. Grace stood beside her.

DAN CANNON CITY'S YOUNGEST ALDERMAN proclaimed the headline and right below was a picture of Charley's childhood friend, and sometimes date, smiling broadly on the steps of City Hall. She remembered the article. It was a fluff piece she'd written at Sherman's request. She'd resented him asking her to use her personal connection to get priority access to the new alderman, but Dan had been a good sport about it—although it had cost her. She'd had to agree to be his partner in a fundraising dance competition. She winced at the memory. She had to soak her feet in ice water and wrap them in cotton for two days straight thanks to the blisters she'd sported from the three consecutive hours they'd spent on the dance floor. It was the fault of those ridiculous peep-toe sling-backs women were expected to wear—and Dan, too, of course. His competitive streak kept them jitter-bugging well after it was clear they had no hope of winning.

"Did you find out who the woman was?" Charley asked.

"The listing says 'Mary Brown'."

"Well, that's not going to be much help, is it?" Charley was disappointed. Finding anything about someone named Mary Brown would be like looking for the proverbial needle in a haystack.

"I'll do some digging and see if I can find anything more for you," Grace offered.

"I'd appreciate it. Thanks." Charley gave Grace a hug.

On her way through the newsroom, she paused beside her old desk to watch the young man—her replacement—hunting-and-pecking at the keyboard of his typewriter amid a cloud of cigarette smoke. He had baby-face features, a soft, round face and light blue eyes. With his hat removed, the combed-over wisps of blond hair stood out on his prema-turely balding head. He wasn't unattractive, but he did have that mama's boy feel about him.

Not exactly top reporter material.

He stopped suddenly and looked up at her. "Can I help you, Miss?"

"Missus. And it's Charley, actually. Charley Hall."

"Charley Hall?" He leapt to his feet, sending the rolling chair back into the filing cabinet behind him. "I thought..." He shook his head. "Never mind."

He'd thought she was a man. Charley smiled. More proof he wasn't up to the job. She held out her hand. "Welcome to the *Trib*..." She glanced down at his typewriter to see his byline—*Lester Pyne*. "...Mr. Pyne. If you have any questions or need someone to show you the ropes, let me know." She wanted to tell him to get out of her chair, but Gran had taught her it's better to kill with kindness than knives. Besides, from what she'd seen so far, he wouldn't last long. She could afford to be magnanimous. That way, Sherman couldn't accuse her of sabotage when she proved who was the better reporter.

"Thanks, but I'll be just fine," he said, resuming his seat.

Just like that, he'd dismissed her. Now he knew Charley Hall was a woman, he didn't have the same respect for the name.

If that's how you want to play it, so be it, Mr. Lester Pyne.

She started to walk away and then paused. *Darn it!* A scoop was a scoop, and she was loyal to the *Trib* even if it wasn't loyal to her. And after all, she'd only promised Marillo *she* wouldn't write anything. "You might want to head down to the Pen. They caught the two guys who shot Kennedy but are holding off making a formal announcement until they've crossed all the t's and dotted the i's."

"How do you know that?"

"Ear to the ground." She smiled sweetly at his astonished expression. "I'd hurry, though. Kingston PD has more leaks than a sieve and you wouldn't want your buddy from the *Whig* to get there first."

Pyne jumped up, sending the rolling chair backward again. He grabbed his jacket off the coat rack, stuffed a notepad into its pocket, and crammed his hat onto his head. "Thanks," he muttered, brushing past her.

"I'll see you in the funny papers," she called after him.

Sherman stood at the door to his office, arms folded across his chest. His eyebrows raised questioningly as she passed, but she simply smiled and strolled out the door. She'd made her point.

Let him stew on that for a while.

She'd gone to Grace hoping for answers, but instead, she'd only discovered more questions. Who was Mary Brown? Who'd killed her and why? And why would she have a picture of Dan hanging in her kitchen? He was a Kingston city alderman; Portsmouth was a separate village.

But the most important question of all remained unanswered. Where was Freddie?

He'd done it to her again!

Charley glared across the church basement at Alderman Dan Cannon, surrounded by a bevy of admiring women. He caught her gaze, winked back at her and returned focus to his harem.

Okay, she conceded, that wasn't fair. They were his constituents and he was—in theory—working. Although she was sure his movie-star good looks—sandy brown hair, strong chin, and tall, athletic physique—contributed to his popularity with the female electorate. And, of course, those eyes—cognac brown, she'd called them, ever since the two had finished a bottle of his father's favourite *Courvoisier* one evening when they were teenagers. She'd felt fine the next morning, but it was obvious Dan was a lightweight in the drinking department. Still was. She glanced around the room. Might explain why he was here now.

Charley had tracked Dan down at his regular job near the waterfront where he was being groomed by his father to take over the family's shipbuilding company. Her plan to find out why a murdered woman would have pinned an article about him up on her wall was stymied, first by Diana, his over-zealous assistant—whom Charley was sure harboured a not-so-secret crush on her boss—and then by Dan himself.

"Hey, Charley, are you here to see me? Sorry, can't talk right now. I'm already late for a meeting with a developer," he'd said when he saw her waiting outside his office. "But why don't we meet for dinner?"

She'd agreed, and he told her he'd send a car to pick her up. Giving Diana a self-satisfied smile, Charley walked backward to the door and almost bumped into Dan, who'd paused on his way out.

"And do you think you could put on a dress?" he'd asked.

"Perhaps," she'd replied, ignoring Diana's snort. "But you better make it worth my while."

Charley glanced down at the teal-and-white organdy party dress she'd chosen and silently cursed Dan for not being completely forthcoming about dinner. She was definitely over-dressed for a church basement dinner-meeting of temperance women.

She returned her attention to her other dinner companion. Dan's mother, Rose, was probably the only other over-dressed woman in the room. But then, Charley had never seen her without her blonde curls sculpted into perfect finger waves or in a dress that hadn't come from Montreal's Holt Renfrew and Company. She'd arranged for her son to speak to the group, although Charley wasn't quite sure why. Rose wasn't a teetotaler herself. She was, however, actively committed to her son's political advancement. His continued bachelorhood was a subject of great concern to her, as she liked to remind Charley.

"Tea?"

Charley glanced up, surprised to see her friend Fiona holding up a china teapot. "Oh no. No more tea. I'm about to float away." Charley turned to her companion. "Mrs. Cannon?"

Rose shook her head. "No, thank you."

"Have you met Fiona MacDonald?" Charley asked.

"No, I don't believe I've had the pleasure," Rose said, her blue eyes zeroing in on the woman. Charley admired Rose's knack for making whomever she was with feel as if she was the most important person in the room at that moment. Dan had had an excellent teacher.

Charley made the introductions. "Mrs. Cannon is Alderman Cannon's mother," she added for clarification to Fiona.

"I'm going to make the rounds and give the two of you a chance to visit," Rose said, rising from her seat. "Please take my chair, Miss MacDonald."

Fiona grinned and put the teapot down on the table. She dropped down into the seat with a weary sigh. "I was surprised to see you here, Charley."

"Probably not more surprised than me." Charley threw one more murderous glare toward Dan and then turned to Fiona. "I didn't know you were a temperance supporter, Fee."

Fiona's freckled face turned pink. "I'm not. I stopped by the church to say a wee prayer for my Da when Minister Monroe asked if I'd like to help out this evening. He said I could bring the wee ones, too, and we'd all get a fine meal out of it."

Charley smiled sympathetically at the young woman who'd had to assume responsibility for her two younger siblings after the death of their father a few years earlier. Their mother, she knew, had died of fever during the crossing over from Scotland over a decade before.

"I dinna think I'd have agreed if I'd known the subject

of tonight's meeting," Fiona continued, her voice hardening. "I think there are better ways to help those afflicted with the drink than promising them salvation or threatening them with hellfire and damnation."

Charley was taken aback by the fierceness in Fiona's tone. "You don't think the work of Mr. Wilson and his AA contemporaries is helpful? I've read they've had tremendous success with their program." In her search to find a way to help her brother, Charley had discovered the Alcoholics Anonymous program and she had hoped to convince Freddie to take part in the local group that met every day in Kingston.

"Alcoholism is not a moral failing, Charley. It canna be 'cured' by prayer alone. It is a physical affliction and must be treated as such."

"Like in a hospital? With doctors and medicine?"

"Yes. Science is the way of the future, just you wait and see."

Charley didn't doubt her. If there was one thing Fiona knew, it was science. Charley had met her a year ago while researching a series of stories for the *Trib* on advances in antibiotics—Mary Barber, a woman pathologist from Britain, had published a paper on how some strains of a common bacteria had become resistant to penicillin. The science was all gibberish to Charley and finding a male researcher who wouldn't condescend to her had been impossible. Fiona worked as a laboratory assistant in the medical faculty at Queen's University and audited as many courses as she could. She was Charley's number one source for information on medical science.

"How is Freddie?" Fiona's question may have seemed like a change of subject to anyone listening to them, but Charley had shared her concerns about her brother's drinking with the woman once she learned it was alcohol that had taken the life of Fiona's father.

Frustration tightened Charley's stomach. "The same."

"Poor lad."

Charley ignored the ladies tittering over another one of Dan's anecdotes. Perhaps the evening wouldn't be a dud after all. Since she was here, maybe she could put her time to good use and tap into Fiona's medical knowledge. She leaned in. "Are you familiar with bullet wounds, Fee?" The small size of Mary Brown's wound and the tremendous amount of blood had been bothering Charley.

Fiona blanched. "Am I what?"

"I came across a murder, earlier today," she whispered.

Fiona's eyes widened. "Just stumbled into it, did ya?"

"Well, not exactly. I was looking for someone. But here's the thing. There was only a single, small bullet hole, but a huge amount of blood, and it was splattered everywhere in the room, not only around the body. How is that possible?"

"When was this?" Fiona swallowed heavily, clearly shocked.

"Earlier this afternoon." Charley was surprised by Fiona's reaction. She was sure one of her jobs was to prepare dead bodies for medical students to examine and practice upon. But as she followed her friend's gaze to the corner of the room where her brother and sister were carefully stacking dishes, she understood. "Oh, you don't have to worry. It wasn't anywhere near here."

Fiona took a deep breath. "The amount of blood would depend on where the bullet entered the body," she said, adopting her professional tone.

"Around her neck."

"Ach, well, it could have hit the carotid artery. That

would explain why there'd be so much blood. The artery would pump out the blood until the heart stopped."

"An artery. That's not a very big target, is it?" Charley mused, leaning back in her chair. "A lucky shot, I guess."

"Or an expert marksman."

"It was most likely a woman." Charley said, recalling the bloody footprints at the house. She doubted there were many women who could aim and shoot with such precision at what would likely have been a moving target. "How long would it have taken for her to die?"

"She'd likely have bled out in under ten minutes. She'd have been unconscious before then, though."

"Less than ten minutes?"

"Aye. Give or take. Not the nicest conversation for a church dinner."

"I didn't realize you were so squeamish, Fee." Charley grinned at her friend.

"Most of the bodies I get are well-dead." She shrugged. "Unlike you, apparently. If you arrived shortly after she, ah, expired, you likely just missed the murderer."

"Murderer? What murderer?" Dan's voice was clipped. "What the heck have you got yourself involved in now, Charley?"

She hadn't noticed him cross the room. "So now you want to talk to me?" She could be snappish, too. "Do you know Fiona MacDonald?"

Fiona stood and shook Dan's hand. "We haven't had the pleasure," she said. "But I've heard and read," she glanced at Charley, "a lot about you."

"The pleasure is mine, Miss MacDonald."

Charley rose, wincing as her high-heel shoes pinched her toes. "Thanks for your help, Fee. I'll see you soon." She turned to Dan. "Now, Mr. Alderman, if you are finished here, can we finally talk?"

"My dear, Miss Stormont, I am all yours."

"Hall," she said, stiffly.

"Of course," he grinned, not even having the decency to look chagrined at being called out for his intentional error. "*Mrs.* Hall."

He led her up the stairs from the church basement to the waiting automobile. It was a family car—the city would never provide such an extravagance to its aldermen. Rose was already seated in the front, which meant Charley was relegated to the back seat.

Great. Another delay, Charley fumed as she listened to Rose and Dan dissect how the evening went.

While Dan accompanied his mother to her front door, Charley moved to the front passenger seat. Dan slipped in beside her and started the engine.

"Now, what did you want to talk to me about?" he said, backing the car out onto the street.

If she was going to get any information from Dan, she knew she'd have to tell him everything. "First, you cannot tell anyone this. It can't get back to Gran..." She took a deep breath. "Freddie's been gone for three days. I was looking for him in Portsmouth and came across a woman who'd been murdered."

"You just 'came across' her? Was she lying in the street?"

"No, of course not. I found her in her kitchen."

"For heaven's sake, Charley. Did you know her? What were you doing in her house?"

"The last time anyone saw Freddie, he was with her."

Dan let out a long breath. "You don't—"

"No, of course not! Freddie couldn't kill anyone no

matter how drunk he was. Besides, it looked like a woman's footprints in the blood."

"Jeepers, Charley!" The car swerved. Even in the dim glow from the streetlights, his skin was visibly greenish in pallor. "Did you call the police?"

She shot him her best evil eye. "What do you take me for? Of course, I called the police."

"So, how can I help?"

"It's the woman. Mary Brown. She had that article I wrote about you earlier this year hanging up in her kitchen. Did you know her?"

"Charley, really!" They'd arrived at her house. He pulled into the driveway, shut off the engine and leaned back against the leather seat. "I know at least a dozen Mary Browns."

"She looked to be late fifties. Greyish-brown hair."

"That could be any one of a thousand women. Besides, I don't represent Portsmouth."

"But she had a purplish mark on her left cheek. It looked like someone had slapped her, but it was a birthmark."

It was only a fraction of a second, but she was sure she'd glimpsed shocked recognition cross his face.

"Doesn't sound familiar," he said slowly. "But I meet hundreds of people every month. I couldn't say for sure if I've met her or not. And as for why she'd have kept an article about me? Honestly, Charley, it could be as much related to you having written it as to me being the subject of it."

He had a point. She hadn't considered that. But Charley was certain she had never seen the woman before today. Unfortunately, she couldn't say the same for Dan.

"I just want to find Freddie," she said.

"Have you filed a missing person's report?"

"No. I don't want that kind of publicity. If the *Whig* ever got hold of—"

His snort cut her off.

"What's so funny?"

"You. Don't you see the irony in you constantly exposing the trials and tribulations of others in your newspaper, while at the same time vigorously guarding your family's privacy?"

"It's not the same thing at all. I only go after public figures. Freddie is sick. He needs help. I'm really worried about him."

Dan turned serious. "Point taken. And I'm sorry. What can I do?"

"I'm going back to Portsmouth tonight. Come with me. Help me look for Freddie."

Dan glanced at his watch. "It's pretty late, and that's not the best area to be in after dark. I think you should wait until morning."

"By morning, he'll be sleeping it off somewhere. If I go tonight, I can probably find him drinking in one of the taverns."

"The ice is finally off the lake. I need to get up early to get in a few hours in my scull before my day starts."

A star rower in university, she knew Dan had started training again in the hope of being selected for the Canadian team that would compete at the London Olympics in July.

"You're picking your boat over me? Please, Dan, it's only one night. I recall a time when you had no trouble staying up all night and still made it to practice on time."

"It's not a *boat*. It's a scull. Jeepers, Charley, after all these years, I'd think you'd know that by now. And I'm not as young and foolish today as I was back then." He raked his hand through his hair and sighed deeply. "You know I'd do anything for you—"

"But?"

"You don't know what you're asking. I just left a group of temperance women and now you want me to accompany you to a bunch of sordid taverns by the lake. How would it look if anyone saw me? You're all for protecting your family's privacy, but this could hurt my career."

Her shoulders slumped. She'd been hoping to leverage his attraction to her in order to help Freddie. It was probably for the best, though. She shouldn't lead him on. "I understand."

"Are you upset with me?"

"No."

"Disappointed?"

She gave him a small smile. "Never."

He moved closer to her and took her hands. "You mean the world to me, you know that, don't you?"

"Dan, please don't." She tried to pull her hands back, but he held on tightly. This was precisely what she hadn't wanted to happen. "We've been friends since we were kids."

"Which is why we'd be so perfect together. You just have to give me a chance."

"I can't," she whispered. "You know I can't." Dammit, a tear slipped from the corner of her eye.

He released her hands and raised a finger to catch the droplet as it landed on her cheek. "Not now, maybe. But some day."

7

SHE WAS BEING FOLLOWED.

A dark shape extracted itself from the wall of the building across the street as she left Beaupre's Tavern, her first stop in her search for Freddie. Several times she stopped to look around, to see if it was following, but she couldn't see anyone. Still, she couldn't shake the sense he was there.

In the shadows.

Waiting.

She'd had to cross her fingers behind her back when Dan made her promise to wait until morning to go to Portsmouth to search for her brother. Going alone was dangerous and a woman wandering the streets in this part of town was only inviting trouble.

But what choice do I have?

Freddie's life was at stake. Besides which, she'd taken precautions. She'd dressed in dark, bulky clothing, and had wrapped her hair in a scarf before tucking it up under a toque to keep it hidden. She'd also made sure she walked with heavy, rolling steps, much as she'd imagined a man who'd had too much to drink would.

The streets weren't exactly deserted. And it wasn't completely quiet, either. But both the occasional straggler walking along the street or a burst of raucous laughter tumbling out from an open window held an ominous quality that only escalated her tension the closer she got to the lake.

The fetid water and decaying fish made her eyes water, their putrid odours mingling with the musty smell of stale hops and acidic tannins from the breweries and tanneries that had been abandoned years ago.

The taverns here were no longer real taverns. The last two she'd entered had been derelict warehouses, co-opted for the purpose of providing cheap liquor for the night. The proprietors and patrons all knew Freddie, but no one had seen him in days.

She clung close to the buildings as she made her way down Yonge Street, her gaze darting back and forth, looking for her stalker. Another drinking house was up ahead, but she'd have to cross the street. Once inside, she'd feel safer. Less exposed. Ironic, considering the clientele.

She took a deep breath, expanded her chest and straightened her shoulders. Striding in a masculine-like swagger, she crossed the street.

So far, so good.

It had to be well past midnight by now. Once she made it inside, she might as well stay until dawn. Unless she could find someone she trusted to walk her home. And really, how likely was that?

She'd just stepped onto the curb when the door to the converted saloon swung open and two men exploded out, fists swinging. Several more followed them into the street, catcalling and hissing. A large woman emerged, calmly stepping past the observers, to douse the fighters with a bucket of water and a few choice words of profanity.

Charley was close enough to receive her own fair share

of spray from the water and she leapt backward to get out of its path only to hit something hard. Something that shouldn't have been there.

A hand wrapped around her waist and another covered her mouth. She struggled against him, but he was too big. Panicking as he hauled her up into his arms, she swung her feet wildly, making contact with his shins. He lowered her to the ground and began to drag her along. She dug in her heels, but that barely slowed his pace.

She tried to scream against his palm, but she could only emit pitiful grunts. His hand slackened for a second as he seemed to readjust his grip. She took the opportunity to bite it. Hard.

"Goddammit, woman!"

He slapped his hand even tighter against her mouth and pulled her into the alley.

"Don't scream," he whispered against her ear. "I'm going to remove my hand now. I want you to be calm."

Calm? Was he kidding? He'd just kidnapped her. Dragged her into an alley for who knows what nefarious purpose. And he expected her to be calm?

"Okay, now, take it easy." Slowly, he lowered his hand from her face and released his grip on her waist.

Charley turned to face him, fists ready to pummel him, feet ready to kick him where it would really hurt. The scream she'd been about to issue froze in her throat as she found herself staring down the barrel of a .38 Special.

"Mrs. Hall, please, calm down." His voice, no doubt meant to be soothing, was rough, like sandpaper across her ears—almost as if he hadn't spoken in a long time.

He knows who I am!

Her heart was racing. In all the years she'd worked for the *Trib*, she'd gotten herself into her fair share of jams with people who'd been angry about something she'd written, but never had she faced anything like this. Never had she been so afraid in her life.

The clouds had cleared, and the just-past-full moon provided considerable light. He wasn't all that tall—maybe five-ten. But he was broad. Powerful. He was wearing a dark overcoat and a dark felt hat with its brim pulled low to cover the top part of his face. She couldn't see his eyes, but his nose looked slightly off-centre and his mouth was set in a stern line. She lowered her gaze to the gun. "Who are you? What do you want?"

"First things first. I need your word you're not going to start screaming your fool head off if I lower my gun."

Her brain was trying to figure out if she could make it out of the alley before he had time to raise it again, take aim and fire. Her legs felt like lead and she could barely catch her breath. Escape was unlikely. "Fine."

"Fine, what?"

Really, he was going to make her say it? No point crossing her fingers this time. She knew she was going to keep to her word. "Fine, I won't scream if you lower your gun."

He nodded and pushed up the brim of his hat. He pocketed his pistol and peered at the hand she'd bitten. "Have you had your rabies shot?" he asked, holding up his hand for her to see where her teeth had left red welts.

It gave Charley a small sense of satisfaction to know she had injured him. He still had the upper hand, but she didn't feel quite so powerless now. "Okay, I lived up to my end of the bargain. I haven't screamed. Now, tell me who you are and what you want? And how do you know my name?"

He reached into his pocket and withdrew a black leather wallet and held it out to her. "My name is Mark Spadina. I'm a detective with Toronto PD."

"You're a cop?" She grabbed the wallet and examined the badge. She didn't know if it was real or not. She'd only ever seen the Kingston version. "What are you doing attacking women in the middle of the night?"

46

"What are you doing wandering the streets in this area of town in the middle of the night?"

"I'm looking for someone."

"Me too."

"Are you looking for Freddie?" Charley couldn't imagine what trouble her brother could have gotten into that would involve a police force a hundred and fifty miles away.

"Who's Freddie?"

Charley exhaled, the first real sense of relief she'd felt in hours. "If not Freddie, then who?"

"Why don't you tell me about Freddie first?"

She'd dealt with her fair share of cops. He wasn't getting off that easily. "Why don't you tell me how you know who I am and why you're following me, *first*?"

Spadina leaned nonchalantly against the wall eyeing her up and down. He looked relaxed but she sensed the tension in him, a spring on a mousetrap that would release with any movement from the intended prey—and she was that prey.

"All right, Mrs. Hall, I'll tell you what you want to know," he said, finally. "I went to your house earlier to speak with you. Your lovely housekeeper advised me of the late hour and told me you were indisposed for the remainder of the evening. I decided to find a nice patch of grass and wait until morning to speak with you, since I took you to be a respectable woman who would not take kindly to being confronted by a stranger in the middle of the night. Imagine my surprise when I saw you get dropped off by that dandy—who I assume is not Mr. Hall—in his fancy car."

"I resent the presumption of your tone!"

"My apologies, ma'am. Don't mean to offend. I just can't help wondering what Mr. Hall would think of you

47

traversing seedy lakeside taverns in the middle of the night. Unless he is the Freddie you mentioned you were looking for."

"He is not. And I assure you, Detective, Mr. Hall would be out here with me, looking for Freddie—" Charley swallowed the lump in her throat, "—if he could." Darn it! He'd distracted her. Such a transparent ploy, but she'd fallen for it. "Why do you want to speak to me? And what is so urgent you couldn't wait until morning?"

"As I was saying, I was about to settle down for the night, assuming you were all snug in your bed when I saw you sneak out of the house. I was curious, so I decided to follow you."

"And attack me."

"Well, I was pretty sure I'd been made. You're good, by the way. Very observant. It's not often I'm caught out." He flashed her a smile.

He had good teeth—she'd give him that.

"I didn't want you thinking you were in jeopardy," he went on, "but I was afraid you'd scream if I approached you, and I really don't want to draw a lot of attention."

"And your solution was to drag me into an alley?"

"The fight provided the perfect diversion, and it seemed like a good idea at the time." He held up his injured hand. "In hindsight, though, it could have been executed better."

"What did you want to talk to me about?"

"You found a body not far from here, earlier today."

Charley felt some of the tension leave her body. Now, it was starting to make sense. "Yes. A Mary Brown."

"Nope."

"Excuse me? We checked the records. The house is owned by Mary Brown."

"Could be, but the body you found was Marjorie

48

Dixon. Brown hair? Fifties? Ugly birthmark on her face? Kind of looks like she lost a fight?"

"Yes, that's her. How did you know about the body? You must have left Toronto not long after I found her?"

"We have a province-wide reporting system. And yes, I've been tracking her for years, so as soon as I got the alert, I came down here."

"You've been tracking her, but you didn't know she was in Kingston?"

"Why don't I walk you home while we continue this conversation," he said, pushing himself off the wall. "She is from Toronto. Until I got the report today, I had no reason to believe she wasn't hiding somewhere in the bowels of my city."

"What did she do to make you want to find her?" Charley's thoughts returned to Freddie. He was last seen with her. "Is she dangerous?"

"Depends." His reply was annoyingly cryptic.

Charley stopped walking, forcing him to do the same. "Is whatever she's involved with what got her killed?"

Spadina shook his head. "I can't say for sure. I don't know what she was doing in Kingston or how long she'd been here."

"But why were *you* looking for her?"

He took her arm and compelled her to resume walking. "She's a grifter, a con artist, a former prostitute who upped her game to prey on older, wealthy men. I've been tracking her for years. Now, it's my turn. What were you doing with her, Mrs. Hall?"

The question startled her. "I didn't know her. I was looking for my brother."

"This is the Freddie you mentioned earlier, I presume?"

She hesitated, reluctant to tell him the rest. It was going

49

to come out, though. Marillo was thorough. It wouldn't be long before he found the connection to Freddie. "The last time anyone saw him, he'd left Beaupre's Tavern with her."

"And you discovered no trace of him when you found the body?"

"No. None. I can't imagine he'd be involved in her murder. He's a loving, sensitive soul."

"Wealthy?"

She could see where he was headed, but it didn't make sense that Mary Brown—Marjorie Dixon, or whoever she was—would have been conning her brother. "He doesn't quite fit the profile, does he? I mean, yes, he has money—some, but Gran has significantly limited his access to it since he returned from the war. He's..." She took a deep breath. "He is having some trouble adjusting to his return. And he's not old. He's only thirty-one."

Thirty-two on Friday.

"How long has he been missing?"

"Three days. Four, now, I guess."

They'd arrived at her home and stood on the sidewalk at the base of the driveway. "I'll wish you a good night, Mrs. Hall. We will talk more tomorrow."

"I don't know what else I can tell you. Have you spoken with Constable Marillo of the Kingston PD? He's the one handling the case."

"I will."

She started up the driveway, paused, and turned back to him. "You're not planning on camping out across the street, are you? Now we've spoken, you'll go to a hotel or boarding house to sleep."

"I'm so pleased you're concerned for my welfare, madam." He grinned. "Rest assured, I will be quite comfortable on that patch of grass over there." His dark eyes crinkled at the edges and his whole face seemed to change with that one smile, going from menacing predator to...what? Non-menacing predator?

Really, Charley, you're being ridiculous.

He was a law man. She had no reason to be afraid of him. And yet...

"Good night, then." She turned and continued into the house. The knowledge the detective was playing sentry did not bring her any comfort.

SERIOUSLY?

Charley turned from the dining room's front window. "Chantal, did you deliver breakfast to Detective Spadina across the street?"

Chantal looked up from the table where she was setting out the breakfast cutlery. "Only coffee, *Madame*."

"But the good china?"

"Well, since it was at *Madame* Stormont's request, I didn't think she would be pleased if I used the staff dishes." She flushed uncomfortably. "Did I make an error?"

"No, it's fine." Charley turned back to the window and watched as Spadina took a sip from the priceless Limoges teacup, and then raised it up in a salute to her.

She didn't know why he was still hanging around, but it was obvious he wasn't going to leave until he continued their conversation from last night. "Set another place at the table, please, Chantal. Since Gran already knows he's out there, we might as well invite him inside."

Charley threw open the front door and motioned for Spadina to come into the house. In the hallway, on their way to the dining room, she whispered, "Please, don't mention to Gran that Freddie is missing."

"She doesn't know?" he whispered back.

"I'll explain later."

Chantal took the teacup from Spadina as they entered the dining room and hurried back to the kitchen.

"You can sit here." Charley motioned to a chair along one side of the table.

"Set for four, I see." Spadina winked conspiratorially as he lowered himself onto the chair. "Will Mr. Hall be joining us?"

Charley stumbled and was caught by Gran as she swept into the room.

"Of course, for four," Gran said. She nodded at Spadina, who'd leapt to his feet, then gave Charley's arm a gentle squeeze of support. "Charlotte, will you go up and tell Freddie I expect him to join us for breakfast?"

"I'd let him sleep, Gran. He was out quite late last night. He'll be along eventually. In the meantime, let me introduce Detective Mark Spadina. Detective, this is my grandmother, Elizabeth Stormont."

With his attention focused on Gran, Charley took the opportunity to examine the detective in the daylight. He was younger than she'd thought. Maybe mid-to-late-thirties. His colouring was too dark to be handsome in the traditional sense. His hair was almost black and worn a little too long, his eyes were a little too piercing beneath heavy black brows, and the unshaven stubble along his cheeks and chin gave him a menacing look. Even though his suit was rumpled, he didn't appear disheveled. Instead, he radiated an arrogance that commanded respect. He was intimidating and imposing, the type of person you wouldn't want to cross paths with in a dark alley. She stifled a giggle.

"A pleasure, ma'am." Spadina bowed his head and gave Gran a million-dollar smile with those perfect white teeth.

And with that smile, everything about him changed. His

eyes, Charley realized, weren't the inky black she'd originally thought. There was a hint of brown to them, like the deep rich coffee she enjoyed so much in the morning. The furrow between his brows vanished, the creases at the corners of his eyes seemed to indicate he'd discovered some secret joke. His jaw, his shoulders, his whole body relaxed. Once again, the predator was gone, replaced by a simple gentleman—no, he'd never be that refined. Replaced by a vigorous man taking a few moments to enjoy a leisurely breakfast.

There was something about this new Mark Spadina that tugged at Charley's memory. Something familiar about him, but she couldn't say what it was. She was certain she'd never met him before last night.

"So, you're the fellow who likes to sleep under the stars, are you?" Gran said, frowning her disapproval.

"Only last night, Mrs. Stormont. I needed to speak to your granddaughter, and I didn't want to disturb the household."

Gran turned to Charley. "What have you gotten yourself into now?"

Crimson heat flushed Charley's face. "It's just a story I'm working on."

"Harrumph." Gran sat down, giving Charley and Spadina leave to do so, also. "I thought you'd decided you weren't going to take Mr. Sherman up on his offer to write for the women's pages, which means you shouldn't be working on any story." She reached for the coffee pot and filled her cup half full, adding a generous amount of cream.

Charley frowned. "I haven't made up my mind yet, and until then, I consider myself gainfully employed by the *Trib*."

Chantal returned with a platter of eggs and sausages.

She moved quickly and efficiently from person to person, filling their plates. Her hands shook more pronouncedly when she served Gran. *Poor girl.* Charley revised her estimate of Chantal's employment down to a month.

Gran peppered Spadina with questions while they ate. The detective's answers provided very little information. As good as Gran was at getting people to talk, he was better at keeping his secrets. In the end, he revealed nothing more to her grandmother than he had to Charley the night before. He was a detective with the Toronto Police Department, and he was in Kingston to follow up on the murder of a woman he'd been tracking for some time.

It was unfortunate, though, Gran now knew she had discovered a dead body.

"What on earth were you doing in Portsmouth?" Gran's eyes narrowed.

"Following up on the prison break yesterday. The guard that was killed lived there." She glanced at Spadina and caught a flicker of admiration in his eyes. Was he impressed with how easily the lie came to her? Well, the best lies were based on a foundation of truth, and she *had* gone to see where the guard lived.

"You found a body in the dead guard's house?" Gran pressed.

"No, of course not in his house. I was following a lead when I came upon it in another house. That's all. Really, Gran, there's nothing for you to worry about."

"It's just all so unsavoury. I will be happy when you're done with all the unpleasantness of the city pages."

"I think we should get going," Charley said to Spadina. "I'm going to take Detective Spadina to the police station," she added for both Spadina and Gran's benefit.

"I wouldn't think he'd need your help for that," she replied.

Charley agreed wholeheartedly, but she couldn't think of another way to get him out of the house and away from Gran's probing questions. "It's simply a courtesy, Gran. I know the officers on the case."

Spadina expressed his thanks for breakfast as Gran accompanied them to the foyer.

"Wait here," Charley said. "I've got to run upstairs to get my pocketbook."

"And while you're up there, speak to your brother," Gran said. "He's sleeping his life away."

Charley nodded. Pretending to speak with Freddie would be a good cover while she telephoned Grace to ask if she could find any information on a Marjorie Dixon, originally from Toronto.

"WHY DON'T you want your grandmother to know your brother's missing?" Spadina asked as they crossed the street to his car.

"It'll only worry her." She allowed him to help her into the passenger seat. "Why do you want to speak to me? I told you everything I know last night. You'll likely get more information from Constable Marillo."

"I'll speak to him, too." Spadina put the car in gear and drove along the waterfront to City Hall. They didn't speak during the ten-minute drive, and it only occurred to Charley as he pulled to a stop in front of the prominent neoclassical building that he didn't know exactly where to go. The city's police department was housed in the market wing, at the back of the complex.

"It's a little over the top, don't you think?" Spadina said, nodding toward the building.

The massive structure, complete with a landmark dome, occupied a full city block, facing Lake Ontario.

"Not when you consider Kingston was the capital of Canada when it was built in 1844," Charley countered.

"Typical Toronto elitist," she murmured under her breath.

"I heard that." Spadina flashed her a grin and her annoyance abated.

"Good." She hopped out of the car, not waiting for him to come around and open her door.

"I can take it from here," he said.

"I think I should go in with you."

"Naw, I'm a big boy. Besides, there may be aspects to the case we don't want civilians—or the media—to know about."

"I'm not going to write about it, if that's what you're worried about. As long as Freddie is missing—" She stopped herself. She didn't know why she was arguing with him. She wanted to be rid of him. But could she trust him not to mention Freddie to Marillo? It was one thing if the Kingston Police figured out the connection on their own, but she didn't want to hand them the information. "Please don't mention Freddie. He's not involved."

"He may have been the last person to see her alive. And he's missing."

"He didn't kill her."

"You're sure about that?"

She squirmed uncomfortably under Spadina's piercing gaze. She knew Freddie hadn't killed the woman, but she couldn't say for certain he wasn't involved in some way. Her gut clenched at the thought that her brother himself might have been injured—or worse—at the time of the murder. She quickly pushed the horrible possibility away. There was no evidence to indicate Freddie had been in the home when Marjorie Dixon was attacked—only that he had left the bar with her the previous evening. She squared her shoulders and tried to stare down Spadina. "He's not a murderer. Besides, the bloody footprints belonged to a woman."

"Or someone with small feet."

"Freddie's over six feet tall. Trust me, his feet aren't small."

Spadina chuckled and threw his hands up in defeat. "Okay, I won't bring up your brother's name. But how are you going to find him? You're not planning any more late-night excursions to Portsmouth, are you?"

She frowned. She'd done what she could in the village last night. There was no point in going back. She'd left her telephone number and a little incentive at each tavern she'd visited, along with the promise of more if they would contact her should Freddie show up. "No trips planned," she conceded.

"That's good to know. I wasn't relishing another late night of babysitting. I do need my beauty sleep." He stepped back, dodging her attempt to slap him. Grinning, he tipped his hat. "I'll leave you now, Mrs. Hall, but I'll be in touch, I'm sure."

She watched him mount the stairs and disappear into City Hall.

The arrogance!

She crossed the street to the park and sat down on a bench to wait. She couldn't quite put her finger on it, but something about Spadina seemed off. And it wasn't just that he never did explain why he'd waited all night to see her again this morning. A mere five minutes later, her suspicions were further heightened as he exited the building by the front entrance, got into his car and drove away. He would barely have had time to find his way through the building to where the police department was located, never mind discuss the case with anyone.

What is he up to?

She crossed the street, wandered up Brock Street and around to the Market Square entrance of the police station.

"Mrs. Hall, what can I do for you this fine morning?"

Charley looked up at Sergeant Kearn who was manning the front desk. They all knew her at the police station, and she knew them. The desk sergeant's job, she was sure, was to stymie any attempt she made to get information from the officers. Jerry Kearn took his role seriously. "I'd like to speak with Constable Marillo. I found the body in the case he's investigating."

"Ah, the Portsmouth murder," Kearn said. "The *other* Portsmouth murder."

"Well, technically, the murder of Mr. Kennedy wasn't in Portsmouth," Charley said. "Unless..." Panic choked her. Had there been another murder? Freddie? No! If Freddie was dead the police would have contacted his family. He was a prominent member of society. Unless there really was some connection with Marjorie Dixon...

"Technically you are correct." Kearn interrupted her dark thoughts. "I guess that's what makes you such a good reporter." His tone was sarcastic.

She closed her eyes, issued a small prayer of thanks and drew in a deep breath.

"Constable Marillo isn't here right now. Is there some message you'd like me to give him?" Kearn asked.

So maybe Spadina's quick exit wasn't unexplained after all. Being overly suspicious of everything and everyone was an occupational hazard for a reporter.

"No message. I was simply curious if any progress has been made on the case."

Kearn looked down at his desk and shuffled through some papers. "Portsmouth, April 26. Yes, here it is. Mary Brown. Most definitely foul play." He looked up and smiled. "And that is all I can say on the matter."

Mary Brown?

Then again, suspicious minds can yield intriguing results.

CHARLEY PAUSED on the front step of her home. *I really should buy myself an automobile.* She blew out a breath. *Of course, it would help if I learned to drive first.*

She'd walked from City Hall to the *Tribune* and then back home again. And while she enjoyed the fresh air and sunshine of the April spring day, the four-mile hike left her anxious, her fingers itching to get onto her typewriter's keyboard.

But what could she write? Grace had been able to access a Toronto prostitution arrest record for Marjorie Dixon, but it was thirty years old. And despite pouring on the charm, Grace couldn't persuade the Toronto Police Department to divulge any information about its investigation into the woman's grifter activities, nor had the officer volunteered any information about cases the department was working on to which she was linked. That wasn't surprising.

What was surprising, however, was the fact that, almost twenty-four hours after the murder, Kingston PD was still unaware of the victim's real name. Shouldn't Toronto PD have advised them of that? After all, her death was important enough to have sent one of their detectives to follow up on it.

Grace promised not to give up. Charley loved that about her. The archivist was as tenacious as a terrier with a bone. She almost felt sorry for the Toronto officer who would be assigned to deal with the archivist's dogged determination to uncover what she could about Marjorie Dixon.

In the meantime, Charley would contact the coroner's office to see if he planned to do an autopsy. It was pretty obvious Marjorie Dixon had been killed by a gunshot to the neck, but sometimes an autopsy was called for in cases with little other evidence.

Her visit to the *Trib*'s office hadn't been entirely pleasant. Lester Pyne's preening over his scoop yesterday—compliments of Charley, not that any recognition had been given to her—had set her on edge. The man was an imbecile. Why couldn't Sherman see that?

She heard voices from the drawing room as soon as she stepped into the foyer. Not in the mood for chit-chat, Charley tried to slip quietly up the stairs to her own room without being noticed. Unfortunately, Gran's hearing was still exceptional.

"Charlotte, do come in and join us."

Chantal appeared, scurrying from the kitchen to take Charley's coat, hat and pocketbook from her. The young woman seemed perpetually flustered.

"It's all right, Chantal, you don't have to rush to greet me when I arrive home. I am perfectly capable of disencumbering myself."

"But *Madame*, I mean, Mrs. Stormont..."

"Yes, of course, when Gran returns from being out, you must definitely run as fast as you can to help her."

She watched the young woman climb the stairs and, once again, downgraded her estimate for how long she'd be around.

Hurry up and come home, Freddie. I have the inside track on this one.

"Ladies," Charley said, entering the drawing room. She bent to kiss her grandmother's cheek and turned to greet the guest. Her smile slipped slightly when she saw Rose Cannon, then she bucked herself up. She wasn't Bessie Stormont's granddaughter for nothing. "Mrs. Cannon. How lovely to see you so soon after last evening."

Chantal reappeared with a teacup for Charley and started to pour from the teapot on the sideboard. Charley was sorely tempted to ask for sherry but was afraid it would set the new housekeeper's world spinning even further out of control. She accepted the cup and sank down into the moss-coloured *bergère* armchair. She had claimed it as her own when she was a teenager and had spent countless hours curled up reading in it. The *bergère* was the only one of its kind in the drawing room. It had a deeper and wider seat than those of the three regular *fauteuils* arrayed around the coffee table. Charley kicked off her shoes and tucked her feet up under her bottom, ignoring her grandmother's scowl. *Not proper deportment for a lady*, Gran would lecture her later. *And especially not in front of a guest.*

But Dan's mother wasn't just any guest. She knew Rose and Gran had been angling for a marriage ever since...well, at least openly since the end of the war. What she really needed was for Rose to see her as a less-than-favourable candidate for her son's hand.

Charley listened as the two women discussed the Daughters of the Empire, smiled sweetly when Gran again suggested she might like to join, and promised Rose she'd consider it when the other woman pressed.

"Well, I must be going." Rose stood. Thank you, Bessie, for the tea. It is always wonderful seeing you." She briefly took the older woman's hand and then turned to Charley. "Charlotte, would you see me out, please?"

Surprised, Charley followed Rose into the foyer. Rose took her coat and hat from Chantal and handed them to Charley to help her. Chantal's dismissal couldn't have been more obvious.

"That was a lovely evening last night," Rose said.

"If you call eating ham and mashed potatoes in a church basement while watching Dan glad-hand half the female population of Kingston a lovely evening…"

Rose's cornflower-blue eyes narrowed, and her mouth pursed.

Charley feared she'd gone too far and had offended the woman. "I'm sorry, Mrs. Cannon. That was entirely inappropriate of me. Yes, it was a lovely evening."

She nodded. "And a worthwhile cause."

"I guess so."

Rose turned so Charley could help her with her coat. "He's a politician with a bright future. It's important he spends time in the community, building rapport with his constituents."

"Of course."

Rose turned to face her. "He said you asked him about a woman while he was taking you home. A Mary Brown?"

"Yes, do you know her?" Charley asked, startled by the change of topic.

"No, I don't know anyone by that name."

"What about Marjorie Dixon?" Charley was sure she saw Rose blanch, but the older woman recovered quickly.

"I don't believe I'm familiar with her, either." She paused to take her hat from Charley and placed it on her head. "I understand the woman in question is dead. Murdered?"

"Yes."

"I'd rather you didn't involve Dan in this. He has a reputation to maintain."

"Did he tell you why I questioned him about her?"

"No, and it doesn't matter. I accepted some time ago that you feel the need to work as a reporter for your grandfather's newspaper, but I hope you won't fight Mr. Sherman and will seriously consider the offer to move to the women's pages. It's just not seemly for a young woman with your pedigree to be mucking around in all this unpleasantness. And I don't want Dan dragged into it, either."

Charley wasn't surprised to learn she'd been a topic of conversation, but it irked her that her grandmother would share news of her demotion so freely.

Rose took her pocketbook from Charley, withdrew a gold-coloured cylinder, and attempted to balance the clutch while removing the top of the lipstick tube.

Charley's eyes widened. Inside the opened pocketbook she could see a folded piece of newsprint.

Get a hold of yourself, Charley. It could be anything. A recipe. An announcement. Don't be so suspicious.

"Let me hold that for you," she said, taking back the pocketbook. She angled the purse, trying to get a better look at the clipping tucked inside, but it was impossible to see what it was.

Finished with applying a fresh coat of lipstick, Rose held out her hand for her pocketbook. As Charley handed it to her, it slipped from her grasp and fell to the floor, spilling its contents onto the hard tiles.

"Oh, how clumsy of me." Charley bent down to retrieve the items. Her heart was banging in her chest. She quickly replaced the items in the clutch, stood and handed Rose her pocketbook, managing to surreptitiously tuck the news-paper article into the pocket of her trousers.

After Rose left, Charley slowly began to unfold the paper. *It couldn't be. It just couldn't.* There were hundreds of articles Rose could clip from the newspaper to carry around with her. And a very good reason she would have kept this particular article about her son. And yet...

With each fold, Charley's heart sank deeper into her chest. And there it was. The headline: *DAN CANNON CITY'S YOUNGEST ALDERMAN.* A jagged edge indicated it had been ripped apart from where the masthead and date would appear.

But there was no blood on it.

Charley leaned heavily against the wall. Was it the same article? The only way to know for sure would be to go back to the scene of the murder and compare the two halves. Was she up for that?

She took a deep breath. Was she really thinking Dan's mother might have killed Marjorie Dixon?

In her years on the crime beat, Charley had learned a lot about human nature. Mostly she'd learned anyone is capable of anything given the right circumstances and more importantly, people aren't always who they seem to be.

She closed her eyes and thought of Dan, her gut churning uneasily. How much did he know? He said he hadn't known Mary Brown, but she was sure she saw a flicker of recognition in his eyes when she described the birthmark on the dead woman's face. And she'd bet dollars to doughnuts Rose had recognized Marjorie Dixon's name.

"Charlotte!" Gran's voice penetrated her disquiet.

"Coming." She refolded the newspaper article and stuffed it back into her pocket, then rejoined her grandmother in the drawing room. Before taking her seat, she poured herself a sherry. "Do you want one, Gran?"

"Certainly, dear. Rose Cannon means well but is a bit of a busybody. I'm not sure why she came today. She didn't seem to have much to say. A lot of talk about nothing, really."

Charley handed her grandmother a glass and sat down in the chair next to her. "It makes me wonder why you press so hard to unite our families."

Gran laughed. "She's harmless, mostly. And her son is quite a catch. The two of you—"

"Stop, please." Charley took a large sip of the sherry, regretting bringing up the topic. "Especially not this week."

"Oh, of course. I'm sorry, my dear. It was very insensitive of me."

They sat sipping their sherries in silence for a few minutes, then the reporter in Charley took over. "How well do you know Rose?"

"Just through charity events, really. She isn't from my generation. Why?"

"Was she raised here? Did you know her before she married Ted Cannon?"

"Yes, of course, she was. I knew her parents very well. Her father and your grandfather were members of the same clubs."

"What about Ted? Did Grandpa know him? Did my father?"

"No, no. Ted is from Toronto. I think there must have been some connection between his family and Rose's, but I don't remember what it was, if I ever knew. He came here to work for her father at the shipyard when they got married. They were all part of the same social set as your parents, of course, so they'd have known each other, certainly."

"Are they happy? Rose and Ted, I mean."

"What a question to ask. You know I don't partake in gossip."

Charley tried not to roll her eyes. For as long as she could remember, Bessie Stormont had had her finger on the pulse of everything that went on in Kingston society. Her insatiable thirst for gossip may have been part of the reason she'd married a newspaper publisher. Her grandparents had made a formidable pair, just at the time the entrepreneurial class was supplanting the aristocracy, such as it was, in Canada. "Then there *is* something," she pressed.

"Well, rumours mostly. You know how those things are. One never knows if there is anything to them. Ted and Rose had been married for several years but were still childless. Ted seemed to develop a wandering eye, if you know what I mean. Rose's parents were beside themselves. They thought of Ted as a son and had planned for him to take over the business." Gran leaned forward conspiratorially. "He was sent away. Back to Toronto. I thought that was the end of him, but Rose picked up and followed him." Gran leaned back in her chair and took a sip of sherry.

"And?" Charley said impatiently.

She shrugged. "I guess the change of scenery worked. Rose became pregnant in Toronto, and a year later they returned to Kingston, a family of three. Being a father seemed to be what Ted needed to settle down. He took over the shipbuilding business and has become a pillar of the community." Gran eyed Charley over her glass. "Why are you so curious about Rose and Ted's relationship? Are you considering Dan—"

"No, I'm not. I'm simply trying to make sense out of some information I've come across."

"You're not thinking of writing a story about the Cannons, are you? Charlotte, I absolutely forbid you—"

"No, Gran. Nothing like that. I'm not writing anything about them."

"Good. You know I don't like spreading gossip. I was only telling you what I had heard in deference to your friendship with Dan."

"I know." Charley stood and set the two empty glasses on the sideboard.

"Will your brother be joining us for dinner? I missed him earlier. He must have slipped out while I was talking to the new girl about menus for his party on Saturday."

Charley's shoulders sagged. "He said he was meeting friends."

"Well, I certainly hope you've told him I expect him to be here for his party."

"Yes, Gran." She bent down to kiss her cheek. "I have some work to do. I'll see you at dinner."

Charley closed the door to her bedroom and sat down on her bed. She unfolded the newspaper article and stared again at the ragged tear along the top.

So, Ted and Rose had spent time in Toronto. Ted had been philandering, but would he have used the services of a prostitute? Or perhaps he'd known Marjorie Dixon from before his marriage? Maybe Rose had discovered a liaison between her husband and the woman in Toronto, and then when she reappeared in Kingston...

Oh, Charley, that is so far-fetched. A fling with a prostitute thirty years ago wouldn't drive a woman like Rose Cannon to commit murder.

But someone had killed Marjorie Dixon. And the dead woman was her only lead to Freddie.

Charley lay back and closed her eyes. She'd just take a few minutes to collect her thoughts...

She woke with a start, disoriented. The room was dark. How long had she been asleep? She'd only closed her eyes for a few seconds.

She glanced at the clock. *Nine-thirty?* She'd missed dinner. Why had Gran let her sleep so long?

She heard it again. Ringing.

The telephone.

She jumped up and stumbled across the room.

"Hello?"

"Are you the lady looking for the Stormont bloke?"

"Yes!" She took a deep breath to try to calm her racing heart. "Is he there? Can I speak with him?"

"Hold on, lady. First things first. You said you'd pay."

"Yes, of course. Tell me where he is."

"Five hundred dollars."

"What? That's outrageous. I don't have five hundred dollars. I'll give you fifty for your troubles. Just tell me where he is? Is this Beaupre's?"

"I don't think you understand, lady. I have him. And I'll not be giving him back to you unless you pay me, right?"

For the second night in a row, Charley found herself stalking the streets of Portsmouth. At least this time she had a firm destination. And the resolve to bring Freddie home.

She'd talked the caller down to one hundred dollars. She knew there was that much in the family's safe—that, and the British Bull Dog revolver her father had carried during his time as a correspondent in the Great War.

The house had been quiet when she'd left. Her grandmother generally retired to her room after dinner, and she suspected Chantal chose to do the same. At least, the housekeeper hadn't been in the kitchen when she returned the dinner tray that had been left in her room. She'd rehearsed several excuses for both women should they discover her opening the safe or leaving the house—none of them very convincing, so she was relieved she hadn't had to use them.

Mostly, Charley was relieved Gran had insisted she have a private telephone in her room. This wasn't the first late-night call she'd received, and certainly not the latest hour she'd received one. It was the 2-a.m. dust-up at Fort Henry, being used as an internment camp, that had caused Gran to declare, "We need a second phone line."

She paused and looked across the street to her destination: Rockwood Asylum. The caller had said he'd meet her at the gazebo near the northeast entrance. Hands in her pockets, her right hand firmly wrapped around the handle of the revolver, left hand clutching the banknotes, she crossed the street and slipped through the stone entrance gate onto the property.

She easily located the gazebo. She'd played here many times as a child. In the past, Rockwood's limestone architecture and beautiful grounds had been a source of civic pride, even appearing on postcards around the turn of the century. It wasn't uncommon for families to enjoy a Sunday picnic on the grounds. But as attitudes toward the mentally ill changed, Rockwood had become more isolated in order to provide patients a sanctuary from the outside world, as well as to keep them away from the rest of society.

"I'm here," she called out when she reached the base of the steps to the wooden gazebo.

"Let me see the money," the voice from the phone whispered from behind her. "Don't turn around. Just hold it out."

As she started to withdraw the bills from her pocket, a flash of black crossed her vision and an arm tightened around her neck. The money was snatched from her hand and she was pulled back against a hard body.

"My brother..." she choked out against the constriction of her throat. He was big and his other arm wrapped around her, forcing her arms down and thwarting her attempt to pull out the gun.

"I'm sure he's fine. Likes the liquor, that one, don't he?"

Her head was spinning, as a hazy curtain descended over her vision, making her loosen her grip on the handle of the revolver.

You've done it now, Charley...

Gran would be so disappointed when neither she nor Freddie made it to the birthday party she was planning.

Just as she couldn't fight the blackness any longer, the pressure was lifted from her neck. Like a rag doll, she slumped down, a grunt echoing in her ears. Hers? Or maybe it had come from the two figures she could dimly make out scrambling on the grass next to her. A hard thump reverberated on the ground and there was a sudden expulsion of air.

Charley took a deep breath and rolled over. Snapping out of her lethargy, she reached into her pocket for the Bull Dog and trained it on the brawlers.

She knew she should run. One had tried to kill her. The other? She had no idea who he was nor what his intentions were.

She staggered to her feet and stood over the men.

"Stop!" she yelled.

The men paused, both turned to look up at her.

"What are you doing?" She recognized the voice.

The other man, the one who had lured her here, leapt to his feet and stumbled off.

"Aren't you going to follow him?" Charley asked.

"What's the point?" Spadina countered, dusting the dirt off his knees as he rose to his feet. "He's just some low-life trying to make a buck."

"He said he's got Freddie. And he's got my money."

Spadina reached out a finger and pushed down the muzzle of the revolver. She hadn't realized she still had it trained on him. "First off, you know he doesn't have Freddie. If he did, he wouldn't have tried to kill you once you gave him what he was asking for. It really wasn't the smartest idea to be waving around all that moolah last night and promising more. There are—"

"Second!" She wasn't in the mood for a lecture.

"Second what?"

"You said first, so I'm assuming there's another point you want to make."

Even in the darkness, his teeth glowed white with his grin. It irritated her even more.

"And second, I have your money. I pulled it out of his hand before I hit him." He reached into the pocket of his coat and took out a handful of banknotes. "But I think I should keep it as payment for saving your life."

"I thought you were a cop," she said, grabbing the money from him. "Saving lives is your job." She stuffed the money back into the pocket of her coat.

"Aren't you going to count it?" He snickered.

"Do I need to?"

Spadina threw back his head, his laughter echoing off the wooden gazebo. "You are the most stubborn, most infuriating, most intriguing woman I have ever met."

"I'll take that as a compliment."

"You should."

"What are you doing here, anyway? Wait! Don't tell me you decided to sleep on the grass across the street again. Can't you afford a hotel, Detective? Don't they pay cops in Toronto?"

He sighed, took her arm and they walked toward the street. "I may have been driving by your house when I saw you sneak out again. And quite frankly, Mrs. Hall, a 'thank you' wouldn't go amiss at this point. That is, unless you want to change your mind and pay me for my services."

She paused and looked up at him. The corners of his eyes were creased with humour. *Talk about infuriating.* "Thank you, Detective," she said in her sweetest, most refined voice. "Regardless of the reason you ended up here, I am most grateful."

"And you are most welcome, Mrs. Hall." He made a small bow, took her arm again, and they continued walking in silence.

"You can call me Charley," she said after a while.

"Certainly. And if you want to be less formal, you can call me Mark when we're alone."

"But 'Detective' when anyone else is around?"

"I do have a professional image to uphold."

A DEEP MALE tenor rumbled from the dining room as Charley descended the staircase the next morning.

Freddie! Relief tinged with irritation—but mostly relief —coursed through her and she quickened her pace.

But the dark hair and broad shoulders of the man seated at the table didn't belong to her brother.

"So nice of you to join us, Charlotte," Gran said when she spotted her in the doorway.

Mark pushed back his chair, rose to his feet and turned toward her. "Mrs. Hall," he said.

"This is becoming quite a habit, Detective." Charley swallowed her disappointment and gave free rein to her irritation.

Mark followed her around the table and pulled out the chair for her. "Your grandmother is very gracious," he said, returning to his seat across the table from her.

"Hmm." She reached for the coffee urn.

"I am surprised you slept in so late, considering you went to bed before dinner last evening," Gran said. "I hope I can count on you for dinner this evening. You know I hate to eat alone."

"Yes, I'm sorry."

"Your brother's room was empty again this morning."

"Yes, he's gone to Belleville for a few days. With friends." Charley had devised the excuse while she was dressing. Gran was too perceptive to continue to believe Freddie's absence was simply a matter of conflicting schedules.

"Oh? When did he leave?"

"Last night. After you had gone to bed. I was returning my dinner dishes to the kitchen when I saw him packing his duffel bag. I told him I'd let you know." She'd practiced the story over and over before coming downstairs and hoped it sounded convincing.

"But he will be back for the party."

"Of course. He wouldn't disappoint you, Gran." *At least not knowingly.*

"Well, I am sorry to leave you before you've eaten, but I really must finish reading my book for book club this afternoon."

Mark rose as Gran got to her feet. "What book are you tackling this month, Mrs. Stormont?"

Charley could have sworn she saw her grandmother's cheeks glow pink. "It's by a talented young American, Truman Capote. It's a coming of age story, set in the South."

Charley couldn't stifle the snort but didn't comment. Gran gave her a disapproving glance.

"It sounds interesting. Perhaps, I'll read it." Mark gave a small bow as Gran passed him on her way out of the room. "What is so funny about your grandmother's book club selection?" he asked when he sat down.

"Nothing. It's actually quite broad-minded." Charley tried to remember who all was in Gran's book club. Most were friends from her suffragette days, and all were now widows, like Gran. She wondered if they'd have chosen the semi-autobiographical, semi-scandalous *Other Voices, Other Rooms* if they hadn't been. "So, Detective, what are you doing here?" she asked, staring at him over the rim of her coffee cup.

"I have a favour to ask of you."

She waited.

"I'd like you to accompany me to the morgue to view the body."

"Why?"

"An autopsy isn't going to be performed. Apparently, Kingston PD doesn't think it's needed. But I thought, as you found her, you might be able to provide more information that might help in catching her killer."

"I've told the police everything I know. They arrived shortly after I did, and I didn't touch anything. Surely, you'd be better off getting answers from them."

"I know how police view things. You're a reporter. You might have noticed something they didn't."

Mark's request frustrated her. It was pointless and would only delay her search for Freddie. She had planned to go back to where she'd found the murder victim and compare the newspaper article she had taken from Rose Cannon to the ripped masthead. She didn't know what that would prove, except that Rose had been there at some point. But while she was there, Charley hoped to speak to some of Mary Brown/Marjorie Dixon's neighbours. They'd likely have been reluctant to speak to the police, but they might be willing to talk to another woman. Maybe one of them had seen Freddie and could give her a lead on where he might be.

On the other hand, she was still confused as to why Mark had left the police station so quickly yesterday. Why hadn't he told Kingston PD the real name of the victim?

Maybe it would be worthwhile spending some time with him today.

"Fine, I'll go with you. We can head over there as soon as I've eaten."

She picked at her breakfast, watching the detective as he slathered a generous amount of butter on the now-cold toast. She couldn't figure him out. When he was focused on a task, such as he was now, he looked dangerous—not someone she would want to encounter on a dark street. She choked on her coffee. Except, she reminded herself, she had encountered him on a dark street—several times.

His eyebrows raised questioningly, and she flushed and lowered her gaze.

Then there were times, mostly when he smiled, when he seemed almost a gentleman, someone she would expect to encounter at one of the social events her grandmother insisted she attend.

"Excuse me, *Madame* Charley." Chantal gave Mark a wide berth as she came around the table to hand her a note.

Charley glanced at it. "Have them wait in the drawing room, please." She took a final sip of coffee. "Apparently, constables Marillo and Adams want to speak with me. Do you have an idea why?"

Mark shook his head. "They're here? Now?"

"Yes, let's go see what they want."

"I'm sure they don't want me intruding on their conversation with you. I'll meet you at the morgue when you're done," Mark said.

Mark's hasty departure contrasted sharply with Charley's slow progression from the dining room to the drawing room. The two men rose when she entered, and she waved them back down. She didn't offer coffee. Gran would be displeased, but Charley saw no need to prolong the meeting with forced niceties.

"Do you have news? Have you found the killer?" she asked.

Both men looked down uncomfortably at their shoes. "No ma'am," Marillo replied.

"I'm not sure how I can help you," Charley said.

"We were hoping to speak with your brother, Frederick," Marillo said, "but your housekeeper says he's left town for a few days."

Charley pushed away her annoyance with Chantal for giving out information about the family. Gran would be furious if she knew. Charley would have to have a word with the girl about the need for discretion when dealing with anyone, even—or in this case, especially—the police.

"We wanted to speak with your grandmother, too," Adams added. "But apparently she's too busy to see us."

"Yes, she is working on a project and has a tight deadline. I am sure I can help with whatever you need." She turned back to Marillo, knowing he'd found the connection between Freddie and Marjorie Dixon, but feigning ignorance. "Why do you need to speak with my brother?"

"The last time anyone saw the victim, she was with him."

"It's interesting that your brother was last seen with her and you found her body," Adams added almost gleefully.

"Coincidental, maybe, but hardly interesting," Charley said. "My brother often goes to Portsmouth and, as I told you at the time, I was investigating a lead for a story."

"What story?" Adams asked.

She shrugged. "It doesn't matter. It didn't pan out, so I dropped it."

"You expect us to believe you dropped a story involving a murder?" Adams probed.

"Well, without knowing who the murderer is or any idea for a motive, it's not much of a story. Do you care to provide a comment?"

"No comment," Marillo snapped.

"I understand you didn't feel the need for an autopsy," Charley pressed, hoping to divert the focus away from Freddie.

"No need," Adams said. "It was obvious how she died. In fact, we've already released the body to Queen's medical school. In all likelihood, she was simply a prostitute who ticked off the wrong person. Maybe your brother."

Charley glared at the constable but didn't bite at the bait he dangled in front of her. "I very much doubt she was a prostitute," she said, again shifting the focus from Freddie back to the victim. "She seemed too well-off, well-dressed, well-cared for—and that house... Not the type of house a prostitute would live in. Is that all you've got on her?"

"Well, we know Mary Brown wasn't her name," Adams said defensively.

"Obviously!" Were they playing games with her? What were they really after?

"Why don't you tell us what *you* know, Mrs. Hall?" Marillo asked, taking back control of the interview.

"All I know is what Detective Spadina told me. He must have told you the same thing."

"Detective Spadina?" Both constables sat up straighter.

"Who is that?" Marillo asked.

"Mark Spadina. From Toronto. He came here right after the murder went out on your provincial... whatever it is you use to communicate between police departments." Charley looked from one man to the other. Marillo had taken out his notepad and started writing. Adams seemed to be taking more time to process what she had said. "He said her real name was Marjorie Dixon and she's a grifter from Toronto—he's been tracking her for a number of years." Charley was starting to get a very bad feeling in the pit of her stomach. "He said he was working with you."

Marillo lowered his pen. "I can assure you, Mrs. Hall, no detective from Toronto is working on this case."

Dɪᴅ Dᴇᴛᴇᴄᴛɪᴠᴇ Sᴘᴀᴅɪɴᴀ—or whoever he was—kill Marjorie Dixon and was he using her to keep abreast of the investigation? Charley didn't know what Spadina's game was, but she sure as heck was going to find out.

She followed the directions given to her by the flustered medical student and descended the stairs to the basement of the Richardson Laboratory. The building, situated adjacent to Kingston General Hospital, was home to the pathology department of Queen's University. She was there because Marillo and Adams had told her Marjorie Dixon's body had been donated to the university for student research. Spadina would figure it out for himself when he tried to find Dixon in the city's morgue.

Charley was livid. She'd always believed herself to be a good judge of character—able to spot a fraud from a mile away. But Spadina had played her. She hated that she now questioned everything that had happened to her over the past forty-eight hours. He'd targeted her that first evening—he hadn't denied it. But she should have been more suspicious when she saw him duck out of the police station yesterday. And was it really a coincidence he happened upon her last evening, seeming to rescue her from the man who tried to steal her money? Or had he orchestrated the whole thing to build her trust?

A door farther along the corridor opened and two men sporting dapper suits stepped out, followed by Fiona. They appeared to thank her before heading down the opposite end of the hallway.

Charley's eyes narrowed as they disappeared into the stairwell. One of the men looked awfully familiar...

"Charley? Is that you?"

Charley waved at her friend and hurried toward her. "Who were those men who just left? I'm sure one of them was Edward Cannon. Am I right?"

"I only know the principal of the university." She shrugged. "The other man? I dinna know."

"You remember the alderman from the temperance dinner, Dan Cannon? Well, the gentleman who left with the principal of Queen's University was Edward Cannon, Dan's father."

A furrow formed between Fiona's eyebrows. "Ach, yes, I remember the alderman—and his mother. But I dinna think that man today could have been his da."

Charley was confident in what she'd seen but decided to drop the subject. "I understand you have the body of the murder victim I discovered."

"Popular lady," Fiona said. "The two gentlemen were here to see her, too. Do you want another wee look at her, then?"

"If you don't mind."

"Nah, it's no bother to me. Come on in." Fiona held open the door to the large, grey room.

"Sorry, I'm late," a deep male voice called from behind Charley. "Oh good, Mrs. Hall, you found her. I, unfortunately, went to the city morgue first."

Mark trotted up to them, not nearly as out of breath as Charley would have hoped. What arrogance to show his face here as if nothing was wrong! She'd give him a piece of her mind.

"Detective Spadina?" Fiona's tone held both surprise and recognition. "I wasn't expecting to see you here."

"You know him?" Charley asked.

"Ach, yes. We met..." Her eyes fell to the floor.

Mark placed a gentle hand on Fiona's shoulder. "I'm sorry to be bringing back bad memories for you, Miss MacDonald. I had no idea you'd moved to Kingston. How are your brother and sister coping?"

Fiona looked up at him and smiled slightly. "They be fine. We all are. Thank you."

Mark gave her shoulder a squeeze and then turned to Charley. "I met the MacDonald family in Toronto, a few years ago."

"When my da died," Fiona supplied.

"So, you really are a cop?" Charley felt as if the ground was constantly shifting beneath her feet. If she moved to the left, the ground tilted right.

"Let me guess, the good constables denied all knowledge of me."

"Yes."

"I suppose I shouldn't be surprised. It can't be pleasant for them to know someone else has been assigned to their case. How much did you tell them?"

"Pretty much everything you told me."

"But nothing about your brother being missing, I assume." If a tone of voice could issue a scolding, his certainly did. He was evidently annoyed she'd revealed his secrets but kept her own.

"Freddie?" Fiona's head whipped toward Charley. "What's he got to do with any of this?"

"Nothing," Charley replied definitively. "Nothing at all." The ground seemed to shift again, but she was finding her footing. "You wanted to look at the body, Detective. Let's do it."

Fiona flipped a light switch and the room was bathed in painfully intense light.

"Sorry, I should have warned ye," Fiona said. "It's not very respectful of the dead, I know, but it needs to be this bright for the students to see what they're doing, you understand."

It wasn't so much the intensity of the light that unnerved Charley as she approached the form lying on a table across the room. It was the smell. The pungent odour of decay brought tears to her eyes and she gagged.

"How can you stand it, Fee?" she asked.

"Ack, you get used to it pretty quickly."

"Somehow, I doubt that."

"No, it's true," Mark said, walking beside her. "In ten or fifteen minutes, you won't even notice it anymore."

In ten or fifteen minutes she hoped to be long gone from this place.

"May I?" Mark asked, pointing to the sheet covering the body. His voice was barely audible above the whirling fans keeping the room chilled.

"Go right ahead," Fiona said.

There was a tremor in his hand as he grasped the edge of the fabric and began to pull it down, revealing Marjorie Dixon's face. The rank odour of death was unleashed in full now and it took all of Charley's twenty-nine years of deportment training from Gran to stifle the gag. Marjorie Dixon's eyes bulged out of their sockets and a purple tongue protruded from her mouth. The crucial birthmark on her cheek was the only thing Charley recognized between the woman she'd discovered murdered and the body lying before her.

Poor thing.

Mark shuddered as if he, too, was shaken by her appearance. He quickly replaced the sheet over her face.

"Don't you want to look at the wound?" Charley asked.

"No," he whispered. "I just needed to make certain it was her." He turned on his heel and bolted from the room.

"That's odd," Charley mused. "You'd think he'd be used to seeing dead bodies."

Fiona shrugged. "Everyone deals with death differently. Let me put madam into a cooler. I'll meet you outside."

Charley couldn't wait to get out into the corridor and the somewhat fresher air, but even there the stench of death seemed to cling to her.

Mark was standing outside the door, his back to the wall, staring up at the ceiling. He didn't seem to notice her.

"So, what happens now?" Charley asked Fiona when she joined them.

"I'd like to arrange to have the body sent back to Toronto for burial," Mark interrupted.

"I'm afraid that's not gonna be possible," Fiona said.

"Look, I know the students need bodies to study, but she's been through so much. The least she should have is a decent burial." Mark's voice rose in anger.

"That's not what I mean," Fiona said. She looked at Charley. "The gentleman that was leaving here as you arrived..." She turned back to Mark. "He's made plans for her burial already. Like you, he just came to see her face. There's a mortician coming to get her this afternoon."

Mark grabbed Charley's arm. "What man?" he demanded.

The ground shifted again. She couldn't deny it any longer. Somehow, the Cannons were involved with Marjorie Dixon.

CHARLEY ACCEPTED Mark's hand as he helped her out of his automobile. She stepped out of the way as he pushed the door closed and pulled her coat tighter to protect herself against the elements. The promise of spring earlier in the week had only been Mother Nature teasing them. Today the sun shone brightly, but there was a frosty chill in the air, especially so close to the waterfront.

"I really think it would be better if I spoke with Ted Cannon alone," she said for probably the tenth time since he'd insisted on driving them to the shipbuilding yard where Dan's father had his office. "He's an old family friend and is likely to be more forthcoming if it's only me."

"I need to be there," Mark replied cryptically, again for probably the tenth time.

"Fine." Charley knew when to stop beating a dead horse. She glanced up at the modest building. The company had been founded by Dan's great-grandfather on his mother's side. It had done very well during the war, but Dan had confided to her that business was slowing down somewhat. But then, it had been the same in the years following the Great War. It would take time for the company to transition back to peacetime pursuits.

Ted Cannon greeted Charley with a smile and a warm

hug. He threw a more cautious look toward Mark. Charley made the introductions but couldn't soften the reality that she had brought a police officer to ask him some questions.

"Are you here on business, too?" Ted turned to Charley, a hurt look in his steel-blue eyes. He was a big man with a broad, friendly face, much like his son's. His once-blond hair had almost disappeared, leaving a few greying wisps circling his skull, like the laurel wreath she'd seen in paintings of Roman emperors.

"Nothing for the *Trib*," she said.

"All right," he said, giving Mark one more critical look before circling around to sit behind the enormous oak desk Charley remembered using as a fort when she and Dan would visit as children. He folded his hands against his chest and leaned back in his chair. "Shoot. What can I do for you?"

Mark went on the offensive before Charley had a chance to speak.

"I understand you were at the Richardson Laboratory this morning."

Ted blanched but didn't deny it. "So?"

"What do you know about the woman whose body you viewed?"

"What's all this about?" He turned to Charley.

"Please answer," Mark barked.

"I am not answering anything until I get more information." He sat forward and gave Mark a glare that would have crippled a less confident man. "Am I under suspicion of something? Do I need a lawyer?"

Charley opened her mouth to reply but Mark spoke first. "Do you think you need a lawyer?"

Charley had had enough. "Seriously, Mark—I mean Detective Spadina. I don't think we need to be quite so confrontational." She ignored the murderous glare Mark threw her way and spoke to Ted. "We are simply looking for more information on the woman. You know she was murdered?"

"You don't think I had anything to do with that, do you?" Ted fell back in his chair as if she'd shot him with a bullet.

Mark held up a hand to stop Charley from continuing. "Mr. Cannon, this isn't how I like to conduct an interrogation—"

"Interrogation?" Ted leapt to his feet. "I think I do need to call my lawyer."

"It's not an interrogation!" Charley scowled at Mark, willing him to back off. Allowing him to accompany her was a very bad idea. She should have tried harder to slip away from him after they'd left Fiona and the lab. Mark was focused on finding a murderer. She only wanted to find Freddie. Even though Ted couldn't possibly have committed the crime—his feet were too large to have left the bloody tracks—the murdered woman was her only, albeit tenuous, link to Freddie. "Let's all sit down and discuss this calmly," she suggested.

"I'll talk to Charlotte, not you," Ted said, lowering himself back into his chair and angling his body away from Mark.

"Thank you." Charley took a deep breath and adopted her I'm-your-best-friend reporter persona. She was a pro at making people feel relaxed so they would drop their guard —plus men tended to underestimate her. "Let's just put out what we all know already. A woman was murdered in Portsmouth. No, Mr. Cannon, you are not a suspect. But you must have known her somehow."

"No, I didn't know her."

"Then—" Mark began.

"Then!" Charley said loudly to drown out Mark's interruption. "Why would you want to view the body?"

Ted glanced over her shoulder as if he was gauging whether or not he could make a quick exit. His brows furrowed as he paused, no doubt carefully choosing his next words. "Let's not play around, here. You obviously know I was there this morning. And you likely know I have arranged a burial for the woman."

"Which is interesting, considering you claim not to know her," Mark calmly injected himself into the conversation, giving Charley a tiny smirk as if to say he could play nice, too, if needs be.

"No, not interesting at all. I was playing golf this morning with the principal of Queen's University—we were part of a foursome; you can check it out. I'll give you the names." He glared at Mark. Then he turned to Charley. "He mentioned the police had sent over the body of a poor woman who had been brutally murdered—donated it, I guess, to the med school." Ted's shoulders lowered and he seemed to become more relaxed. "I thought it was a terrible fate for a woman who had met such an unhappy end. So, I offered—or I should say, my company offered—to give her a decent burial."

Charley looked at Mark. He didn't believe it. Neither did she.

"Did the principal not tell you how important it is to have bodies for the students to learn from?" Charley asked.

"One body isn't going to make a difference."

Charley wasn't so sure. In the past, there had been stories about medical students digging up graves looking for fresh cadavers to autopsy. She hadn't heard of anything similar recently, but murders were rare in Kingston and this seemed like it would be a good learning opportunity for the students.

"But why *this* body?" Mark pushed. "Surely there are other deserving members of society who have met an untimely end? Don't you think they deserve a decent burial? Was it the fact she was murdered? That she had no relatives?" He didn't stop to wait for answers, he kept pressing. "She was from Toronto. Did you know that? I understand you're from Toronto. Is that a coincidence? Maybe you knew her from before—"

"What is going on in here?"

Charley jerked her head around. Dan stood in the doorway, his face angrier than she'd seen in a long time—at least since university when he'd had to rescue a novice rower who'd almost drowned in the Cataraqui River after being the victim of hazing by senior team members.

"We're conducting a murder investigation. Wait outside," Mark said, leaping to his feet.

He and Dan approached one another, stopping within inches of each other in the middle of the room.

"I'd like to see your badge, Officer."

"It's Detective," Mark said and pulled out the leather wallet containing his police shield.

Dan took it from him and examined it thoroughly. Charley held her breath. She might not know what a real police badge looked like, but as a lawyer, Dan most certainly did. She remained suspicious of Mark. She couldn't ignore Constable Marillo's denial that he was working on the murder case, but then again, Fiona had at least confirmed he was a police officer.

"Toronto? You're out of your jurisdiction, aren't you, Detective?" Dan said, handing back the wallet.

"As I said, I'm conducting a murder investigation. I go where the evidence takes me."

"Well, then, I guess it's a good thing I'm here. You don't want to be interrogating suspects without their lawyer present, do you?"

"I didn't think you specialized in criminal law, Alderman. I thought your focus was more in the area of inheritance."

Charley gasped at the blatant insult. How did Spadina know Dan was an alderman or that he was in line to take over the family's shipbuilding business?

"I think you'll find I am quite well versed in all areas of law, order and jurisdiction, Detective."

Charley held her breath as the two men glared at each other. Two dominant males used to getting their way. They bore identical expressions of mutual loathing. Dan was younger and had a couple of inches on Mark, but if they came to blows, Charley would put her money on the detective. She doubted he'd be bound by the Marquess of Queensberry rules or any other code of fair play.

"Your father's not a suspect." Charley moved to stand between the two men.

When he was angry, Dan's amber eyes darkened to deep brown, but they were no match for the simmering blackness in Mark's. With such oversized egos fighting for space, the sprawling office suddenly seemed to shrink.

"Gentlemen, please," Ted said, breaking the tension. "I have nothing to hide. I've told Detective Spadina all I know. We're done here."

Charley placed her hand on Mark's chest to stop him from contradicting Ted. "We should go," she said. She gave Dan and his father a small, apologetic smile and ushered Mark toward the door.

"Charley, wait, please. Can I have a word?" Dan said, throwing a glare at Mark. "Alone."

Charley glanced at Dan. She hesitated briefly and then stepped back into the room. "Don't wait for me. I'll find my own way home," she said, closing the office door on Mark's thunderous scowl.

Charley leaned her head against the closed door. Mark was clearly furious with her, but really, he'd left her no choice. He'd escalated the situation well beyond what was called for. Maybe intimidation got results with the type of suspects he investigated in Toronto, but that approach wasn't going to work with people like the Cannons.

She turned into the room in time to see a look pass between Dan and his father.

"Well, I'll leave you kids to talk. I have a meeting I'm late for," Ted said, somewhat too conveniently to be believed. "Always nice to see you, Charlotte."

Definitely not believable.

After Ted left, Charley watched patiently as Dan paced around the room.

"What are you doing with that guy?" he said, finally.

"That *guy* is a cop. And he's investigating the murder of the body I found while I was looking for Freddie... Remember?"

"Oh jeepers, Freddie. I forgot." Dan's face fell. He reached Charley in two strides and cupped her shoulders. "Did you find him? How is he?"

She shook her head, willing away the tears lurking just behind her eyes. Tears of sadness, for sure, but mostly they were tears of frustration. She was no closer to finding her brother today than she had been when she'd asked for Dan's help two days ago. If anything, more questions were piling up in her brain. And those questions centred on what happened to Marjorie Dixon, aka Mary Brown. For some reason, her search for answers always seemed to circle back to the Cannon family.

"I'm sorry." He pulled her into his arms, and she allowed her head to rest against his shoulder.

She closed her eyes, deeply inhaling his familiar woodsy scent as his hands rubbed small, comforting circles on her back. She angled her head to look up at him and saw his amber eyes darkening. They'd darkened before, when he was confronting Mark. But this time the earthy brown wasn't the result of anger, but of a long-simmering passion. He lowered his head toward her, his mouth getting closer.

"No!" She pushed him away. "Dan, please. We can't. You know we can't."

He stepped back and ran his hand through his hair. "No, I don't know." His voice was rough.

"I should go."

"No, wait. I'm sorry." Dan flung himself down into the chair Mark had been sitting in. "It's just... No, never mind. You're right." He shook his head.

Charley sat in the chair beside him. She was exhausted. "Was there something you wanted to talk about?"

"The woman. The one you asked me about the other night."

"Marjorie Dixon."

"Is that her name? I thought you said it was Mary-something."

"Detective Spadina said Mary Brown was an alias. Her real name is—was—Marjorie Dixon."

"Okay." Dan sounded as tired as she felt. "You were right. I did recognize her. But only because of the awful birthmark she had. You've got to understand, Charley, I get approached by people all the time. It's not reasonable for me to remember every one of them."

"But you remembered her. And not only because of the birthmark," she supplied.

"She came up to me after a temperance rally a month ago or more. Is the date important? I can have Diana look up the information if you need it."

"No, the date isn't important."

He nodded, relieved. "She said she knew my parents—from when they lived in Toronto. That was before I was born. She asked about them. I told her they were well and then I moved on to another person. I didn't give her any more thought until you told me she'd been murdered."

"But you denied knowing her when I asked you. And your father denied knowing her just now."

"I don't know why I didn't tell you the truth when you asked me the other night. I think I was startled that someone I had met had been killed. As for my father, I can only speculate. And please, Charley, you have to promise nothing I've said or will say will leave this room."

"I'm only trying to find Freddie."

"Okay." Dan took a deep breath. "My father grew up in Toronto and had quite the reputation as a lady's man. It's possible, in his youth, he may have had dalliances with...ah, women who were not of the same social standing."

"It must have been quite a dalliance if he's prepared to pay for her burial. But why hide it?"

"I don't know. Maybe he wants to protect my mother. Or perhaps it's nothing more than a man trying to do something nice for another human being and not wanting to have it misconstrued." Dan shrugged his shoulders. "In any event, it's not the type of thing the family wants to see splashed all over the newspaper—especially now."

"Because you're a city alderman?" Charley asked.

"Well, here's the thing." Dan angled his body closer toward her. "I'm hoping to use my success at this summer's Olympics in London to launch my candidacy to become a federal member of Parliament."

Charley's eyes widened. She knew Dan was ambitious, but he wasn't even yet thirty.

"You're surprised."

"Aren't you a little young for such lofty ambitions?"

Dan threw back his head and laughed. "Says the woman who is the same age as me and is fighting to retain her position as the first female city reporter for the *Tribune*. And you wonder why I think we're such a perfect match."

"Which party?"

"The Liberals, of course."

She should have known. The Liberal party had been in power for over a decade. Of course, the riding of Kingston had gone to the Conservatives in the last election. Dan had just enough conceit to believe he could win it back. And, given his popularity, especially among the female voters, he probably would.

"So, now you understand why my parents and I have been reticent to get involved with this case. The woman—"

"Marjorie Dixon." She deliberately hadn't used her name when speaking with Ted to see if he'd volunteer it himself and prove a connection. It didn't matter, now— Charley felt it was respectful to use it.

"Yes, Marjorie Dixon may have known my father in the past but, as you said yourself, he is not a suspect in her murder. So please, Charley, for all our sakes, drop it."

Charley surreptitiously crossed the fingers of her left hand as she promised Dan. Every reporter instinct she possessed was screaming there was more to the story than he was telling her—probably more than he knew himself. While his father may not be a suspect, she couldn't entirely exonerate his mother, Rose.

Marjorie Dixon had most likely been murdered by a woman. And Rose had had that article tucked into her pocketbook. Was it the same clipping torn from the wall at the crime scene? Had Rose visited Marjorie Dixon before she died and argued with her? Worse yet—did she kill her? Would a long-ago affair justify such an act? Or perhaps the affair had been rekindled when Marjorie came to Kingston.

Or, given Dan's future plans, had there been blackmail involved?

And then there was Detective Mark Spadina. His interest in the case seemed to be more personal than professional. Charley had been flabbergasted when Mark told Fiona he wanted to take the body back with him to Toronto for burial, but more so by his reaction when he'd been told he couldn't. Charley believed his excuse about giving some respect to the deceased about as much as she'd believed Ted when he'd said essentially the same thing.

No, there was definitely more going on here. And the more people obstructed her inquiries, the more determined she became. Because somewhere in all of this lay the truth about where Freddie had gone and why he hadn't returned home.

Charley declined Dan's offer to drive her home. That was the last place she wanted to be right now.

Charley loved everything about a newsroom, from the steady rat-a-tat-tat of typewriter keys pressing ink to paper, to the smell of tobacco blending with stale coffee floating through the air, to the beads of sweat dotting the brows of reporters as a deadline fast approached. Most of all she loved the act of writing—searching for the perfect words to make the reader understand the importance of the message she wanted to convey.

She wasn't even gone and she already missed the place —missed being part of the daily hive of activity—missed digging into the story before it became "news."

She'd come back to get her bearings, take a breather and try to make sense out of the information she'd gleaned in the last forty-eight hours. But as she approached the desk that had once been hers, she realized this place had become as unfamiliar as the rest of her life. Someone was sitting in Mama Bear's chair—and he was still there.

"Hello, Lester," she said, trying for a friendly tone. "Working on anything good?"

"Kennedy murder," he mumbled, his eyes glued to his typewriter.

Still?

He'd been here three days and he was still working on the same story? She'd have expected him to move on to something else. Keep up with the case, sure, but there was more going on in the city than that. If she'd been on the city beat—

"Hall!" John Sherman bellowed from across the room. "I'm still waiting for an answer."

"You'll be the first to know when I have one," she called back and then flinched at the door slam.

Lester had stopped typing and was looking at her through rheumy eyes—too much time at the typewriter and not enough out in the field, she decided.

"Is there anything you want?" He sounded irritated.

He'd taken her desk, he'd taken her job, he'd taken her story, and *he* was irritated with *her*? *The very idea!* She bit her tongue and forced a smile—*kindness not knives, kindness not knives, kindness not knives...* "No. Just thought I'd stop and say hello on my way by."

He gave her a curt nod, effectively dismissing her.

At least Grace was happy to see her.

Charley carefully disentangled herself from the younger woman's enthusiastic embrace. "Been a bit rough, has it?" she asked.

"You have no idea," Grace said, rolling her eyes. "That Lester Pyne has no clue what he's doing. Oh, he can write a pretty piece of prose, but for investigation? He has the instincts of a brick. He's constantly in here asking me to do this, find that, but he's only fishing." She sat down on the stool beside her big work table and rolled up her sleeves. "What can I help you with?"

"I'm here to do a bit of fishing myself, I'm afraid," Charley said taking the stool next to her.

"I haven't been able to find anything more on Marjorie Dixon." Grace heaved a sigh.

Charley leaned her elbows on the table. "I'm not sure if there is anything else to find." More and more she was doubting the story Mark had given her. "I was wondering if you could look into Detective Mark Spadina, from Toronto PD?"

"You want to investigate a cop?" Grace asked. "Do you think he's dirty?"

Charley paused. Did she? "No, not dirty, *per se*. But I do think he's hiding something."

"Are you looking for arrest records between him and Marjorie Dixon?"

"I doubt you'll find anything. You said she had nothing more recent than thirty years ago, so he wouldn't have been around then. But find out anything you can about cases he has been involved in—particularly related to prostitution and grifting." There had to be some reason Marjorie Dixon had come to his attention. Maybe it was related to another case he'd been working on.

"Got it," Grace said.

And then there was something between him and Fiona's family. "Also, a death a few years ago, in Toronto, of a man named MacDonald."

Grace looked up from the pad she'd been taking notes on and eyed her incredulously. "Seriously? That's all you're going to give me? Do you know how many MacDonalds there are in Toronto?"

"Cross-referenced with Detective Spadina. I think he was the officer on the case."

"Oh well, then, piece of cake," she said and grinned.

"Also check that none of Marjorie Dixon's arrest records mentions an Edward Cannon."

"The shipbuilding Cannons." Grace's voice didn't hold a hint of surprise. She'd worked with too many reporters on too many *exposés* to be shocked by any request. Grace made the note and then lowered her pencil and raised her gaze to Charley. "I've worked with you for a long time, now. I hope you know you can trust me."

"Of course, I do."

Grace lowered her voice. "This isn't just a story you're working on for the *Trib*, is it? I know you take all your stories seriously, but this one seems much more personal. I want to help you, but in order for me to do that, I need all the facts. I think you're holding out on me."

Charley's shoulders sagged and she sighed wearily. "Only to protect you. I don't want you to lose your job over something you did for me."

"Are you asking me to do anything illegal?"

"No, of course not. But you're right. It's not for the paper."

"Then tell me. Please, let me help."

Charley started at the beginning with her search for Freddie in Portsmouth and left nothing out. As she laid out the facts of the case as she knew them, she began to feel physically lighter, a terrible weight was lifting off her shoulders. In Grace, she had an ally she could trust.

"Thank you. I now have a much better understanding of what you're looking for and why," Grace said when Charley finished her story. "Is there anything else you need me to research for you?"

There was one more thing, but Charley hesitated to open that particular Pandora's box, fearful of what she'd release. Nevertheless, finding Freddie trumped everything, even her relationship with Dan. "I need you to do a thorough search for any financial transactions you can find relating to either Edward or Rose Cannon. Have there been any large commercial transactions or donations recently?" She paused and then forced herself to continue. "And do the same for their son, the alderman."

Blackmail could be a powerful motivator.

CHARLEY HANDED the cabbie the banknotes and accepted his hand as she exited the taxi.

"Are you sure you don't want me to wait for you, Missus?" he asked.

She appreciated the offer. This certainly wasn't the best neighbourhood, but while the houses looked dingy and decaying, it seemed to be more a factor of the inherent poverty of the occupants rather than any nefarious neglect. There were curtains in the windows of the homes and the yards were tidy with well-tended gardens. She got the sense this was a place of permanence for these people, and they took pride in what little they had. There had been curious looks from some of the residents as the cab had driven along the street, as if they weren't accustomed to visitors. But she'd seen nothing hostile in their gazes. "Thanks, I'll be fine."

"Okay," he said, clearly not happy. "When you call in, ask for me, Romeo Arcadi, and I'll come back to get you." He looked around. "Not everyone will come out here, and I don't want to see you stranded after dark."

Charley smiled at the wiry cabbie to appease him. He looked a little like an aging boxer—lean and tough—but she wasn't the helpless dame he thought she was. Still, she did appreciate his obvious concern for her welfare.

She'd called Fiona at the university lab but had been told she'd already left for the day and since she didn't have a home telephone, there was no way to contact her. Grace—bless her—had searched out Fiona's home address.

Charley was stymied. There seemed to be so many unanswered questions in this case, and she wasn't sure where to go next. Marjorie Dixon was her only lead to Freddie. Somehow the Cannons were involved, but so was Mark Spadina. While she didn't feel threatened by the Cannons, she couldn't say the same about the detective. At the very least, she reasoned, she needed to find out more about him and his motive for coming to Kingston.

Fiona seemed her best bet.

"Charley, what brings you here?" Fiona asked, her cheeks turning pink.

"I'm so sorry. I don't mean to intrude." Charley immediately regretted her impulsive decision to come to the woman's home, uninvited. It was obvious Fiona was embarrassed. "You have a lovely garden," she said, trying to put her at ease.

"Ach, well, it's still early days yet, but it's important to have good healthy food for the bairns, you understand." She took a step back. "Do you want to come in?"

The interior was a big, open room with a stove, counter and sink, and icebox along one wall. A large, wooden table with four chairs dominated one end and a sofa the other. There was a single door off to the left which Charley assumed led to a bedroom, or perhaps a toilet. Did it have indoor plumbing? Her heart sank, but she'd be damned if she'd show her dismay to Fiona.

Looking out of place because of its value, not its utility,

an intricately carved cabinet rested against the back wall. Mahogany, if Charley had to guess. It stood at least five-feet tall and had brightly polished brass handles. Even from across the room, the extraordinary workmanship was apparent. Fiona's father had been a cabinetmaker, she remembered. He must have been exceptional.

Another terrible loss to alcohol.

"Can I get you something?" Fiona asked. "The bairns will be home soon, and I need to be getting started on their dinner."

"No, thank you. I won't take up much of your time." She sat on the sofa and indicated for her friend to do the same. "I wanted to follow up on a few things you said earlier today."

"Aye?"

"I am sorry, I didn't realize your father had died under suspicious circumstances."

"Phew." Fiona exhaled in disgust. "There was nothing suspicious about it. He drank himself to death."

"Yes, but Detective Spadina—"

"Oh him. That's what you be wanting to know about, eh?" Fiona grinned. "He's a nice-looking gentleman if you like the dark, broody type. A bit too Heathcliff for me, mind."

Charley's breath caught and she felt her face flame with embarrassment at Fiona's assumption. "No! You misunderstand. That's not why I'm asking." She took several deep breaths to get herself back on track. "If there was nothing suspicious about your father's death, why was Detective Spadina involved? I'm trying to figure out why he's here in Kingston, and what he has to do with Marjorie Dixon."

Fiona rose suddenly and walked over to the sink.

Charley followed. "I didn't mean to upset you."

"Oh, no, you dinna." Fiona turned, a large headless pigeon in her hand. Fiona looked down at the bird and then back to Charley. "I can't afford to be buying meat for the wee ones, you understand."

Charley took a step forward and looked in the sink. Another pigeon and three squirrels. All headless.

"I used to be able to use traps, but the city dinna like that. Afraid for the cats, I suppose." She started plucking the feathers. "I have to cut the heads off before the bairns see them. It's the eyes, you know. Spooks them."

Charley's stomach heaved and her heart broke. She turned to gaze out the front window.

"Anyway," Fiona continued, "you wanted to know about the detective and my da. It was a routine investigation. Just an old drunkard who got lost in the woods north of the city. He'd been staying in a cabin up there. No one knows what really happened. It looked like he stumbled into the lake one night and drowned."

"And Detective Spadina was assigned to investigate?"

"Ach, no. It was a regular constable doing that. I'm not sure why the detective got involved. To be honest, for a while I thought perhaps he had his eye on me, but..." She shrugged.

"Speak of the devil," Charley said, watching Mark round his vehicle, open the back door and retrieve a large cardboard box.

"Eh?" Fiona rushed to her side, wiping her hands on her apron and sending a few wayward feathers fluttering to the ground. "Well, I'll be." She opened the door.

Mark's smile faltered slightly when he saw Charley. "Mrs. Hall, I didn't expect to see you here."

"That makes two of us," Charley replied.

Mark crossed the room and placed the box on the table. "I brought some goodies for the kiddos," he said.

"You shouldn't have," Fiona said, half-heartedly, and then oohed and ahhed with pleasure as she removed a ham, carrots and potatoes from the box and placed them on the counter.

"There's a toy police car and a colouring book with crayons, too," Mark said, helping her unpack the items.

"That's very kind of you," Fiona said.

"I was worried about your family when you left Toronto. I'm glad to find you doing so well here. You've had to take on a lot of responsibility. This," he motioned to the box, "is just a little something to help with the kids."

Charley watched the exchange, feeling inadequate. She'd arrived here empty-handed and looking for information. Mark had come bearing gifts and looking for nothing. It didn't help to realize she'd come to rely on Fiona for her scientific knowledge, using her as a prime source of information, and not once had she thought to compensate the young woman for her time and effort.

Mark turned to her. "So, Mrs. Hall, are you here checking up on me?"

For the second time within a few minutes, her cheeks flamed. "Why would I do that? Fiona and I are friends. Is it so hard to believe I'd stop by to visit?" She winced inwardly. Even to her, her words sounded disingenuous. Fortunately, he didn't press.

"I expect the kiddos will be home soon. We should get out of your way, Miss MacDonald," Mark said. "Mrs. Hall, can I offer you a drive home?"

She was stuck. She didn't want to leave yet. There was still more she wanted to know about Mark, but he was right. They—especially she—were intruding.

Charley sighed and followed Mark to the door. She hesitated, turning back to Fiona. There was one more thing she was curious about. "At the lab, when those men left, you were adamant the man with the university principal couldn't have been Dan Cannon's father. Why?"

"I dinna say he couldn't, did I?" Fiona lowered her gaze and smoothed out the folds of her apron.

"You did."

"I don't like to be speadin' gossip," she said. "I know the alderman is a friend of yours."

"I would never accuse you of gossip, Fee, but I need to know. It's important."

"Okay then. How much do you know about genetics?"

"You know very well when it comes to science, everything I know comes from you."

"Oh aye, that's verra true." Fiona chuckled. "So, here's a little lesson for ye. Genetics are the traits that come to you from your ma and your da. Some of these traits are dominant, meaning they will prevail over the others."

"That much I remember from high school."

"Well, one of these dominant traits is brown eyes."

"So?"

"So, it means that two blue-eyed parents will always produce a blue-eyed bairn, never one with brown eyes."

"Blue eyes. Brown eyes. What was that all about?" Mark asked as they stepped off the front stoop of Fiona's house.

Charley shook her head, still trying to digest the information Fiona had given her. She leaned against Mark's car and took a deep breath. "It means at least one of your parents had brown eyes."

"Could be. I never knew my parents."

She straightened. "I'm sorry."

"Don't be. You can't miss what you never had, right?"

Charley nodded slowly. She had only the vaguest memories of her own parents—a whiff of pipe tobacco would sometimes make her think of her father or the feeling of satin across her cheek, her mother. It was impossible, though. She'd been far too young to have ever noticed those things, and yet thoughts of them always came with a gentle ache of longing. How was it she had barely registered their presence, but twenty-five years after their deaths continued to feel their absence at her very core?

He moved beside her and leaned against the car. "What is it about what Miss MacDonald said about eye colour has you so shaken up?"

She snapped back to the present. "You met Dan Cannon and his father?"

"I was with you this afternoon, remember?"

"Did you happen to notice their eye colour?"

"Among other things. Your Dan has brown eyes and his father, blue."

Charley swallowed, not wanting to acknowledge it, let alone speak it. Gossip indeed. "His mother has blue eyes, too. Do you know what that means?"

Mark let out a belly laugh and slapped his knee. "Sure do. It means your boyfriend is a bastard in pedigree as well as disposition."

"He is not my boyfriend!"

"Oh yes, I forgot the mysterious Mr. Hall."

Anger rose in her, sharp-edged and gaping. "Just forget everything. Go back to whatever Toronto hole you crawled out from."

Mark pushed himself off the car and grasped her shoulders. "Hey, I'm sorry, Charley. I shouldn't have said that. That was going too far."

She shrugged out of his grip, still too angry to accept his apology even if he did look contrite. She concentrated instead on the effect the new information had on their case. If the genetics issue was so obvious to Fiona, how many other people would realize the truth? "Do you think it's possible Marjorie Dixon figured out Ted Cannon couldn't be Dan's father and was blackmailing Rose?"

"And she killed her?"

Charley winced, still having difficulty making that final, logical step. "I need to talk to Rose." She marched past Mark and put her hand on the passenger door handle. "Let's go."

"Whoa, Tiger, let's think about this a bit more. If Edward Cannon is defending his wife, he likely knows his son's a bast—knows he isn't his flesh and blood. But in any event, if they were being blackmailed by Marjorie Dixon, why pay for her burial?"

"That's why we need to talk to Rose. Get some answers." She rattled the handle, impatient for him to get in and unlock her door.

Mark looked at his wristwatch and shook his head. "I don't disagree with you, but I think we should wait until morning."

Morning? Endure another night without answers? Another night worrying about Freddie?

"It's getting late," Mark continued. "Mr. Cannon is probably home now or will be shortly. It would be better if we talked to his wife when she's alone, don't you think?"

Reluctantly, Charley had to agree he made sense.

But Freddie was out there somewhere.

"Besides, you promised your grandmother you would be home for dinner this evening."

She groaned. *Gran.* She'd forgotten. Freddie would have to wait one more night. "Okay, but first thing tomorrow we get answers."

"Yes, ma'am." Mark threw her a mock salute. "Now, I hate to even bring this up, but given our recent history, can you promise me you won't be sneaking off to Portsmouth for a third night in a row? I need my beauty sleep so I can't keep—ow!" He grinned while he rubbed the arm she'd just punched. "I'll take that as a yes. I'm staying at the flophouse on Ontario street. Give me a ring in the morning when you're ready and I'll come get you."

"What? You mean you're not coming for breakfast?" she quipped.

"Why, thank you for the invitation, Mrs. Hall. I thought you'd never ask."

A taxi pulled to a stop beside Mark's car. "Is everything

all right here, Missus?" Romeo Arcadi's poor boy-capped head appeared above the cab's roof. "I thought I'd swing back by in case you needed a ride home."

"You've made your own arrangements, I see." Mark rounded his car and unlocked the driver's door. "Therefore, I will bid you a good night and see you at 8 a.m. sharp tomorrow morning. Oh, and please ask Chantal not to over-cook the eggs. I like mine runny."

"Dan? This is a surprise." Charley stepped into the Cannons' sitting room, Mark right behind her.

"You don't think I saw you crossing your fingers yesterday?" Dan said coming toward them. "You forget how well I know you, Charley." He held out his hand to Mark. "Detective, I guess I shouldn't be surprised to see you here, too."

"Please, everyone. Sit down." Rose moved away from the window where she'd been standing to indicate they should all take seats. "There's coffee and rum cake. There's no reason we can't all have a nice conversation." She lowered herself onto the gold and maroon brocade sofa. "Please close the door, Daniel. I don't want to be interrupted. Charlotte, will you pour?"

Charley sat in the wing-backed chair closest to the coffee service. Mark took a seat across from her and immediately plucked the largest piece of rum cake from the plate. Honestly, the man had just finished an enormous breakfast —runny eggs and all—and he was still hungry? Dan sat beside his mother on the sofa.

No one spoke while she poured them each a cup of coffee, automatically adding the preferred amount of sugar and cream to both Rose's and Dan's cups. She and Mark both took theirs black. The fact she knew everyone in the room so well made her purpose here even more uncomfortable.

Rose's hand shook as she accepted the cup and saucer. She was wearing a simple, unadorned black dress. Charley glanced at Dan. He, too, was in black. Unusual colours for both of them.

"We are burying Mrs. Dixon later this morning," Dan said as if he'd read her mind.

"You're having a proper funeral?" Mark asked.

"It will be small. Just us. The minister from our church will officiate," Dan said.

"All this for a woman you claim not to have known?" Mark didn't attempt to conceal his sarcasm.

Dan opened his mouth to reply, but Rose placed her hand on his and shook her head.

"How can we help you, Detective?" Rose said.

"You can start by being honest with us," Mark said. "You did know Marjorie Dixon, didn't you?"

"Knowing and killing aren't the same thing," Dan said. "First you accuse my father, and now you're here to do the same with my mother. Why on earth do you think anyone in my family is involved in this poor woman's death?"

"Blackmail would be a good motive," Mark said.

Dan's eyes widened in shock and he glanced quickly toward his mother.

"You think we were being blackmailed?" Rose gasped.

"We think that somehow Marjorie Dixon realized Dan wasn't Ted's son," Charley said, throwing Mark a warning glare. He was going too quickly, again. Just as he had with Ted yesterday, he was being too brusque in his accusation. She'd wanted to go slower, to soften the blow.

She turned to Dan, trying to read his expression. Did he know? Oh please, let this not be news to him.

"Why on earth would you think that?" Rose raised her chin defiantly and took her son's hand.

"Well he can't be, can he?" Charley said. She was relieved to see Mark take another piece of rum cake, seeming to let her proceed with the interrogation—no, she didn't want it to become that—the conversation. "Both you and Ted have blue eyes and Dan has brown. Genetics say—"

"Stop, Charley, please." Dan gave his mother's hand a squeeze.

"I'm sorry, Dan. It's impossible for both Rose and Ted to be your parents."

"And you think Marjorie Dixon realized this, was blackmailing us, and so someone—my mother you suspect—killed her? Is this the theory you're advancing?"

Charley nodded slowly. The look of betrayal in Dan's eyes ripped at her soul.

"Jeepers, Charley!" Dan stood suddenly and began pacing the room. "I've known you all my life. Our families have been close. And you honestly believe my mother is capable of murder?"

"I only want to find Freddie," Charley said as if that would make him understand. "Marjorie Dixon was the last person he was seen with." Charley reached into her pocketbook and withdrew the news clipping. She didn't have definitive proof, but she was convinced it was the missing article. "I know your mother was there—at Marjorie Dixon's home, where she was murdered."

Dan snatched the clipping from her hand and turned to his mother. "You never told me about this."

"All right, enough of this," Rose snapped. "Daniel sit down." Her features softened when she turned to Charley. "I am sorry about Freddie. Daniel told me he's missing. I'll tell you what you want to know about Marjorie Dixon, but I'm afraid it won't help you find your brother," she glanced at Mark, "or the murderer."

Rose waited for Dan to return to his seat, then she took his hand. "What I am about to tell you we only told Daniel last evening. You are correct, Charlotte—but only partially. You are incorrect to assume Ted is not Daniel's father. The truth is, I am not his mother."

Dan wrapped his arm around Rose and hugged her. "You will always be my mother," he said, kissing her temple.

"Thank you, darling."

Charley glanced at Mark. He'd put down his plate, his dark brooding gaze focused on Rose and Dan.

"For some reason, Ted and I were unable to conceive a child. It was heartbreaking. We talked about adoption, there are certainly many needy children out there. But there is something about having your own child, your own flesh and blood, to carry on your legacy. It may be an old-fashioned idea, but that was how we felt—how we feel. If I couldn't bear a child, did that mean Ted should be deprived of having one? I didn't want that. So, we made discreet inquiries and through some old contacts of Ted's in Toronto we were introduced to a woman who had been through some hard times but was making a concerted effort to change her life."

"Marjorie Dixon," Charley whispered the name under her breath.

"I never knew her name. I didn't want to. She was paid very well to conceive, bear and deliver our child. After it was done, we returned to Kingston, telling everyone the year in Toronto had done wonders for our marriage and introduced our brand-new baby boy."

Mark gagged and his skin had taken on a greenish hue. He excused himself and hurried from the room.

Serves him right for eating all that rum cake.

"When Daniel described the woman he'd met at a temperance rally some weeks ago, I knew immediately who she was," Rose continued. "I did go see her, to make sure she wasn't planning on making trouble for us. But that was a month ago, and she was perfectly healthy when I left her."

"She wasn't blackmailing you?"

"No, not at all." Rose's voice was confident, but her eyes wouldn't meet Charley's.

"I think she's answered all your questions," Dan said, rising. "I'll show you out."

Charley wanted to press for more, but Dan was right, she'd gotten what she came for. She bent to retrieve the news clipping Dan had dropped and handed it to Rose.

"I'm really sorry about all this," Charley said to Dan as he helped her on with her coat.

"I wish you'd learn to leave well enough alone."

"I need to find—"

"I know. Freddie." He tucked a strand of Charley's hair behind her ear. "I don't like that detective you're hanging around with."

She shrugged. "I'll take any help I can if it means finding my brother."

"I checked him out."

"You have connections with Toronto PD? Even Grace hasn't been able to find out much about him."

"I called in a favour from an old rowing buddy of mine who is now a cop in Toronto. Be careful, Charley. It seems your Detective Spadina is not here on official police business at all. He's AWOL."

ABSENT WITHOUT LEAVE. That's what Dan had said. Mark was AWOL from the Toronto Police Department.

And he'd disappeared again. Just left her at the Cannons' to find her own way home. Charley declined Dan's offer to drive her home and called Romeo Arcadi instead.

"Where to today, Missus?" the cabbie asked as she got into the back seat.

Where to, indeed. With no other leads, she decided to go back to the beginning. She gave Arcadi the Portsmouth address for Mary Brown, ignoring his distressed "tsk, tsk." If he insisted on being her driver, he was going to have to accept she went to some disreputable places.

"Where is everyone?" Charley glanced out the window at the vacant streets as the cab entered Portsmouth. Even the tavern, which she always thought of as standing sentinel to the village, looked deserted.

"At the funeral, I presume," Arcadi said.

"What funeral?"

"Mr. Kennedy, the guard who was killed a few days ago. Most of the city's expected to attend."

How did she not know that? Up until a few days ago, Charley had been current on all the major events going on in her city. She'd have known about the funeral. Heck, she'd have been there. The Kingston Pen murder had been *her* story. She quietly cursed John Sherman and his decision to hand it—and her job—to Lester Pyne, whose only real credential as a reporter was that he was male.

"Did you say something?" Arcadi glanced at her in his rear-view mirror.

"No, nothing." She sighed. The status of her job at the *Trib* was the least of her problems right now. Besides, it was probably for the best she wasn't still working the Pen murder. Without the pressure of a hard deadline, she had the time and space to work on her own investigation. She'd sort things out with Sherman once she found Freddie.

The cab pulled up in front of Mary Brown's house. Whatever police investigation had gone on, it was obviously finished. There was nothing to restrict her from going up and knocking on the bright yellow door.

"I'll wait right here," Arcadi said, helping her from the cab. This time he wasn't even giving her the option of sending him away.

She shrugged. So be it.

She'd expected the house to be deserted and was surprised when the door was opened almost immediately by a heavy-set woman with a long braid of grey hair, warm, hazel eyes and a broad smile. "Hello dearie, can I help you?"

"Are you the owner of this house?" Charley asked. Maybe she'd been mistaken and Dixon hadn't been the owner. Maybe it belonged to this woman and Marjorie Dixon had only been a lodger. If so, did that mean...? "Are you Mary Brown?"

"Well, yes, I am Mary Brown. Come in. You are most welcome here."

Charley followed the woman along the hallway to the

kitchen at the back of the house.

"Would you like a glass of water?" Mary asked as she motioned for her to take a seat at the table.

"No, thank you." Charley was disconcerted as she glanced around the familiar room. It was impeccably clean now. No blood. No flies. The partially torn news clipping had been removed and a vase of fresh flowers sat on the counter. No one would ever suspect a murder had occurred here only a few days ago.

The woman sat in the chair beside Charley and took her hand. "I don't want you to be embarrassed, dearie. You're not the first young lady who's had to fight this demon. I'm here to help."

"What?" Charley pulled back. "I think you misunderstand why I'm here."

"Oh, I'm sorry. You asked for Mary Brown, so I assumed..." She shook her head, clearly confused. "Why are you here?"

"I'm looking for my brother. The last person to see him was the woman who was killed here on Monday—the woman I thought was named Mary Brown, but it turns out she was Marjorie Dixon. I was looking for him when I found her—" She paused, startled as Mary pushed her chair back suddenly and moved toward the sink.

"You were the one who found her? Poor darling."

Charley didn't know who the "poor darling" was supposed to refer to, her or the murdered woman. "You knew her?"

"No, not at all. I only arrived yesterday. I spoke with the police, of course. I needed them to allow me in to begin getting things back in order. But I'd never met the woman who was here before me. I didn't even know her true name."

"But you *are* Mary Brown, aren't you? And this is your

house." She shook her head in frustration. Mark said she was a grifter. Was her presence here simply her latest confidence scam? "Was Marjorie Dixon squatting here? Was she pretending to be you while you were away? Pretending to be Mary Brown?"

The woman's hazel eyes gave her a sympathetic look. "Oh, no dearie, she was Mary Brown. We are all Mary Brown."

"What do you mean 'all'? Isn't Mary Brown a person?"

The woman filled a glass of water from the faucet at the sink and placed it on the table in front of Charley. "Your brother, he is afflicted by the demon alcohol, yes?"

"Yes."

She resumed her seat beside Charley. "Our calling, the Mary Browns, is to defeat the devil that controls the drink. We work in towns and cities across the country. We go where we are needed. When someone is ready to be saved, they need only ask for Mary Brown and we will rescue them."

"You can cure people of their addiction to alcohol?" Was it possible Marjorie Dixon had been helping Freddie fight his addiction? That didn't explain why he hadn't come home.

And why would anyone want to kill someone whose life purpose was to help others?

"Of course, we do it all the time."

"But how?"

"We take away the drink."

She made it sound simple, but from what Charley had seen with Freddie, and from talking with Fiona, she knew overcoming an addiction was far from simple. "I don't understand."

"We take them someplace where there is no possibility

of them getting access to alcohol."

"A hospital, you mean?" Fiona had mentioned the role of medical science in treatment.

"No. Somewhere they can be alone. To pray on a cure. We bring them their food and any supplies they need. But until the demon is beaten, they remain isolated."

"Like in the woods or something like that?" Charley was starting to get a very bad feeling about all this.

"Precisely. We have several secluded cabins up north of Toronto that we use."

Charley held her breath. "What about around here?"

The woman shook her head. "I don't know. That was what Mary—the poor dear—was setting up for us. I guess I'll be starting from scratch to find someplace suitable to do our work here."

A cabin in the woods.

A drowning in the lake.

The pieces were falling into place. Charley felt the same rush of excitement as when she was working on an investigation for the *Trib*. At first, nothing seems to make any sense. Then, one tiny piece of information, appearing almost insignificant, arrives and suddenly everything becomes crystal clear.

Except, in this case, not everything. She still didn't know why Mark was in Kingston nor where her brother was. But she knew who had killed Marjorie Dixon and why. And with any luck, the killer would lead her to Freddie.

Arcadi seemed happier with the address she gave him. While it was true, the university's medical lab was more respectable than the last few places she'd made him take her, it could prove to be the most dangerous.

It had been nagging at her since she'd visited Fiona's home yesterday. All those headless pigeons and squirrels.

Fiona hadn't noticed her yet. She had knocked on the lab's door, but the woman seemed too engrossed in her task to have heard.

"Fee?"

Fiona jumped and she grabbed the counter to stop herself from sliding off her stool. "By Jesus, Charley, you scared the life out of me. What are you doing sneaking up on a person like that?"

"Sorry. I didn't mean to startle you." Charley walked farther into the room. There were four parallel rows of counters, each with five microscopes placed along their lengths. She stopped beside Fiona, who was perched on a stool at the second counter, carefully cutting a sliver of some organ and placing it onto the glass slide she had taken from the small stack beside her. "What are you doing?"

"Getting ready for Dr. Symon's histology class. It's a longitudinal section of a cardiac muscle."

"A heart?"

Fiona looked up and smiled. "Verra good. Soon you won't be needing me to help you with your research."

Charley took the seat beside her and watched, fascinated by the precision with which Fiona carefully dissected the muscle, placed a small portion on a slide, added some solution and then placed another tiny piece of glass on top to secure the sample into place. She repeated the process five more times.

"That's that, then," Fiona said, wiping her hands on her lab coat. She shifted on her stool to face Charley. "To what do I owe this visit? Are you working on a new story?"

"No, same one."

"Ach, then I don't know how I can be helping you. I told you everything I know about Detective Spadina."

"What about Marjorie Dixon?" On the drive to the university, Charley had considered how she'd approach Fiona. She sympathized with her. Fiona held Marjorie Dixon responsible for her father's death. But she was a reasonable person; she wouldn't simply kill someone out of spite. There must have been extenuating circumstances. Maybe self-defense, although there was nothing at the scene to indicate that. Still, Charley was certain if she could just talk to her—reason with her—she'd be able to convince her to do the right thing and turn herself in. Charley would be with her every step of the way.

"I don't know anyone by that name."

"The body, yesterday. The woman we came to see. The one that Ted Cannon arranged to have buried."

She shrugged. "I'm never told their names. They're all anonymous to us."

Was she deliberately being daft? Then again, maybe Fiona never knew her real name. Charley tried again. "What about Mary Brown?"

Fiona's eyebrow raised and her mouth formed a grim smirk. "As I'm sure you know by now, Charley, there is no Mary Brown."

"You know who I mean."

"What is it you're asking me? Though I think you

already know the answers, don't ya. That's why you're here, isn't it?"

"Please tell me what happened, Fee. I can help."

"Just so we're clear. I can tell you what happened, sure enough, but I'll not be needing anyone's help." Fiona had picked up the scalpel and was twirling it in her hand.

Charley tensed. The movement may have looked casual, but she understood Fiona's subtle threat. She quelled the shiver of fear radiating along her spine. She could still reach her friend, make her see the wisdom of accepting responsibility. Nevertheless, it didn't help that she was alone here. Mark, Marillo, Adams—contacting any one of them before confronting Fiona would have been a smart thing to do. But she never imagined she'd be in any real danger, and from Fiona, of all people. "I'm listening."

"Have you ever seen what happens when a heavy drinker stops cold turkey?"

Charley shook her head.

"It's a terrible thing, Charley. A person's nervous system goes haywire. They become anxious, suffer hallucinations, sometimes seizures. Sometimes they even drop dead from heart failure."

"I didn't know," Charley whispered, her fear for Freddie heightened all the more.

Fiona looked down at the scalpel twisting between her fingers. "I guess to make sense of it, I should start at the beginning, aye?"

Charley swallowed heavily and nodded.

"We came to Canada—my da, stepmother, and Sarah and Benjamin. It was my step-ma's idea. She'd heard there was opportunity here and wanted a better life for her kids. Sarah and Benjamin are my half-sister and brother, you ken?" She looked up at Charley, waited for an acknowledgment and then continued. "But fate's a cruel mistress, aye? And she died on the crossing."

"I'm sorry."

"My da took it pretty well, all things considered. After all, it wasn't the first wife he'd buried." Fiona's voice held no emotion and Charley wondered how old she'd been when her mother died. But she remained silent, waiting for the story to continue.

"The first few years in Toronto were good for us. He was an excellent cabinetmaker and was never without work. I took over raising the bairns, for which he was most appreciative. His promise to me was he would pay for me to go to medical school once they were old enough to manage." She gave Charley a sad grin. "You did know that was my dream, aye?"

"Yes, and you'd have been an amazing doctor."

Fiona nodded. "Aye, I would. But the war came and there wasn't much call for fancy cabinets. Da took a job making light machine guns in a factory. He'd always been a drinker, but it was during the war when it began to get out of control. By some miracle, he didn't lose the job, but he quit it the day peace was declared. He was certain things would go back to the way they were before the war. But he also knew he had to do something about the drink. That was when he met her."

"Marjorie Dixon."

Fiona flinched at the name. "Aye, but that was not the name she gave. Mary Brown, she said she was." Fiona's tone was bitter. "*Diabolus*, I say she is."

The Latin term for "devil" Charley noted.

"He brought her around one time. I don't think he expected me to be home—and the young ones were away at school. He gave her most of his money—money that was supposed to send me to medical school in Toronto. Sarah and Benjamin were almost of an age that I could go. I think that was the impetus behind Da's determination to quit the drink."

"But how could he pay for medical school if he gave her most of his money?"

"Ach, now you're getting to the meat of it, Charley," Fiona said. "He was convinced his old clients would return, and he would get more money—enough to support us like before." Fiona's hand tightened on the scalpel. "The money he gave her was a charity, to support her in her good work, and so God would look kindly on him, he said."

"So, she took him to a cabin north of Toronto," Charley said.

"She *abandoned* him in a cabin north of Toronto," Fiona corrected her. "Oh, she'd plan to come by every few days with food, but it was thought that alone in the woods he could pray the alcohol away and once it was gone from his body, the thirst for it would weaken, and he'd be cured."

"Promising salvation or threatening hellfire and damnation," Charley muttered under her breath.

"What was that?"

"It's what you said to me at the temperance supper, remember? Alcoholism is not a moral failing. It can't be 'cured' by prayer alone."

"Yes, I remember."

"And your reaction to my discovering a body. I thought it was strange you seemed a little queasy by my questions."

"It is most unfortunate that it was you who happened across her. From your description, you'd likely just missed me leaving the place."

"How did Detective Spadina get involved?

Fiona shrugged. "It must have been because of the

description of the woman I gave to the police after Da died. It was after that he started coming around. I didn't make the connection until I saw him again yesterday."

"The police never found her?"

"No, she vanished into thin air—not a trace of her."

"Until now."

"I couldn't believe it. Of all the places for her to turn up. I was crossing Market Street, trying to avoid a temperance rally when I saw her. I hid until it was over and then followed her to Portsmouth so I could learn where she lived. I agonized for weeks about what to do. Should I call the police or confront her myself?"

"You never thought of simply leaving things be?"

"No! She needed to be stopped. Who knows how many other deaths she and her kind are responsible for?" Fiona's voice took on a note of desperation. "You have to understand, I dinna go there with the intention of killing her."

"What happened?"

"I tried to reason with her. I tried to make her promise to stop doing what she was doing, but she refused. She wouldn't even take responsibility for Da's dying. She blamed him for not being strong enough. I couldn't take it anymore. She had to be stopped." Fiona's eyes became wild as she stared intently at Charley. "You understand that, don't you? She couldna be allowed to continue."

"But Freddie..." Charley's throat constricted as she fought back tears of frustration and fear. "The last time anyone saw him, he was with her."

"I dinna know that." Fiona seemed genuinely shocked by the news. "If I had, I would have asked about him. Told you right away. Maybe the new Mary will know. They multiply like rabbits. You canna get rid of one without another one popping up."

If that was the case, Charley couldn't help but wonder what logic Fiona had employed to justify killing Marjorie Dixon, knowing she'd simply be replaced. But then, it was more personal than that. She could live with the knowledge that people she deemed as misguided were doing horrible things. It was the fact that this particular Mary Brown had been responsible for her father's death. But just as Fiona had been unable to persuade Marjorie Dixon to stop her work, Charley was now doubting she'd be able to convince her friend to turn herself in.

"I just came from seeing the new Mary Brown. She has no idea where he would be. Marjorie Dixon left no information about any work she'd done since she'd been here."

Fiona reached out with her empty hand and attempted to stroke Charley's hair. She didn't seem to take offense when Charley jerked back in alarm. She simply dropped her arm and sighed. "Then I am sorry, *mo charaid*, but if he's been on his own since Monday, he's likely already dead or close to it."

Charley wasn't prepared to give up on her brother. He'd survived worse during the war.

Hang on, Freddie. I'll find you somehow.

"I am curious as to how you figured out it was me?" Fiona asked.

"It was what you said at the temperance dinner when I suggested the murderer had made a lucky shot. You said it could have been an expert marksman."

"That seems like a pretty big leap of logic, even for your active imagination."

"True, but for some reason, it stuck. And then when I was at your house yesterday.... The headless pigeons and squirrels. It took a while, but I realized if you weren't trapping them, you must have been shooting them. But they're so small, so for them to be edible at all you'd have to shoot their heads not their bodies—that's why they were headless —and to do that, you'd have to be—"

"An expert marksman," Fiona interrupted.

"And someone well versed in anatomy, in the case of Marjorie Dixon. You wanted her death to be quick," Charley added. "When the new Mary Brown explained how they did their work, I made the connection to your father's death."

"So, you understand why I did it."

"I do," Charley said, and she really did. "But that doesn't make it right. You have to turn yourself in, Fee."

"I canna. What would happen to the wee bairns?"

"I'll make sure they're cared for."

"It's a death sentence, they'll be hanging me."

"I'll get you the best lawyer. There are extenuating circumstances that I'm sure the court will take into consideration."

Fiona stood and pointed the scalpel at Charley. "I'm afraid I don't have the same confidence in our legal system. I gave that Mary a chance to stop taking advantage of people who were desperate for help. I'll not be held responsible for her failure to do the right thing."

"What about your responsibility to do the right thing?" Charley stepped off her chair and began to back away as Fiona slowly advanced on her.

"It grieves me, Charley. Have no doubt. You've been a good friend and I am truly sorry to be losing you."

"You won't get away with this." Charley's slow retreat was halted by another bank of counters. Her eyes darted left and right, looking for something to use to defend herself. She lunged toward one of the metal stools and threw it. Fiona nimbly avoided it, but her attention was distracted just long enough to allow Charley to scramble to the other side of the counter. Still, Fiona stood between her and the exit. "This isn't you, Fee. Stop. Think about what you're doing."

"You're wrong, Charley. This is me. You know, when an animal is caught in a trap, they'll sometimes chew off their leg to escape. You're like my leg. I have to get rid of you if I am to get out of this trap I'm in." She circled around the end of the counter.

Charley continued to back away slowly, but she had nowhere to go. In a moment she'd be pressed against a wall, a counter on either side effectively boxing her in.

Who is in a trap now?

"I'll make it painless. I know exactly where to cut. It'll be fast. Like it was with the Mary." Fiona's eyes bore into Charley's. She held the scalpel up in front of her. Advancing closer.

Closer.

Charley couldn't wait anymore. She'd have to act now if she was to have any momentum. She took a deep breath, lowered her head and charged at the woman, catching her in her chest and sending her flailing backward. She heard the clatter of the scalpel sliding along the floor, but she didn't slow down to see if Fiona was able to retrieve it.

She rushed to the door, pulled it open, opened her mouth to scream and ran headlong into something solid and immovable.

"Whoa, Tiger. Where's the fire?" Mark said, grasping Charley's shoulders.

"Fiona... scalpel..." Charley panted as she tried to shove Mark back out of the room.

Faster than she thought possible, Mark perceived what was going on and propelled Charley behind him, unholstered his gun, and stepped through the doorway. "What's going on here, Miss MacDonald," he called.

"Stay back. I won't let you arrest me."

"Come on now, Miss MacDonald. You don't want to do this. Think of your brother and sister." Mark's voice was quiet and calm as he slowly walked toward Fiona. "You don't want them to lose the only family member they have left, do you?"

"If you arrest me, I'll surely hang, and then what good will I be to them?" She'd retrieved the scalpel and held it up defensively.

"That's a pretty big assumption, Miss MacDonald. We both know there are extenuating circumstances here."

"That's what Charley said, too, but I don't believe her. Women like me don't get breaks."

"So, how do you see this playing out?" Mark was getting closer. "I'm not going to shoot you, and frankly, I don't want to have to break your arm to get that scalpel from you, but I will if I have to."

Fiona's eyes darted from Mark to Charley. Charley could see so many emotions flickering across the young woman's face—panic, fear, sadness. Then, without warning, the scalpel fell to the floor and she slumped against the counter.

Immediately Mark was on her. He kicked away the scalpel before pulling her hands behind her back and attaching a pair of handcuffs he'd taken from the pocket of his rumpled overcoat.

"You just happened to have a pair of handcuffs with you?" Charley asked.

Mark turned in surprise and gave her an exasperated look. "I'm a cop. And what are you still doing here?"

Charley opened her mouth to say she was too worried to leave him alone with a killer but stopped herself when she realized how ridiculous that would sound. She turned on her heel and rushed upstairs to the departmental office to call the police.

When she returned, Fiona was curled up in a corner, sobbing quietly while Mark paced the room. He'd removed his overcoat and she saw he was dressed in a well-tailored black suit and tie. He'd also shaved, she realized. It made him look years younger.

"What's the occasion?" she asked.

"Huh?"

"You. You're looking pretty spiffy all of a sudden."

"I went to the funeral."

"Oh, of course, I should have realized." Charley shook her head in frustration. Again, she'd forgotten about the Kennedy funeral. She imagined pretty much every police officer would have attended. "I hear the whole city was there."

"What?"

"The funeral for Mr. Kennedy."

"Mister...? Oh, you mean the prison guard. No, I wasn't at that funeral."

"Then whose?" As soon as she asked, she realized she already knew the answer. She probably shouldn't be surprised given how involved he'd been in the case, but she was having difficulty imagining Mark standing with Dan and his parents as Marjorie Dixon was laid to rest.

"It was a nice service," he added. "Very dignified."

Fiona made a gagging noise and both turned to her.

"What's that?" Mark said, harshly.

"I said it's better than she deserves."

"A decent burial is the very least anyone deserves," he muttered angrily. He spun on his heel and resumed his pacing.

"How did you know to come here?" Charley asked, crossing her arms over her chest. "When did you realize Fiona killed her?"

"I didn't." Mark glanced back at Fiona and scowled. "I came here to talk to her. I tried to yesterday but you were there, so I couldn't."

Ah, so there had been more than altruism to the food and gifts he'd brought with him yesterday. Somehow that made her feel less guilty about her empty-handed visit. At least she'd been upfront about what she'd wanted. Mark hadn't been honest about anything since he'd arrived in Kingston. Since she'd solved his case for him, at the very least, he owed her some answers.

"Why have you been so interested in Marjorie Dixon?" she asked. "You've been pursuing her for years. Surely, she couldn't have been that difficult to find in Toronto. And now you're AWOL from your job to investigate her murder. There's got to be more going on than simply looking for a prostitute-turned-grifter."

Mark leaned back against a counter and eyed Charley. "You're a pretty good investigator, Mrs. Hall. I'm surprised you haven't figured it out."

Her brain hurt. She'd had enough surprises for the day. First learning Marjorie Dixon was Dan's real mother and then that her friend, Fiona, was a murderer. "Humour me."

"Okay." He shrugged. "I told you I never knew my parents. I was raised in an orphanage on Spadina street."

"Spadina? Oh, I see. What about Mark?"

"It was a religious orphanage. We were all named after saints of one sort or another."

"Were you adopted?"

"No. I spent my whole childhood there. I became a cop because I wanted to learn who my parents were."

"And did you?"

"Oh, for heaven's sake, Charley," Fiona blurted out of nowhere. "Of course, he did. I thought you were smarter than that."

"She was smart enough to figure out you're the murderer," Mark said, shooting Fiona another scowl. "But yes, really, Charley, I am disappointed you haven't figured out Marjorie Dixon was my mother."

Charley sat down hard on a stool. She hadn't expected that. "Your mother," she repeated stupidly.

"She was still working as a prostitute when I was born. I later learned she had come into some money and had left the trade. But there were still stories of her with various men, of them giving her money."

"You never met her?"

He shrugged. "I figured I would someday. Once I discovered where she'd gotten her money—who she'd fleeced for it—and what she was doing with it."

"Now it's too late," Charley whispered, her heart breaking for the man who would never meet his mother. At least Mark now knew where the money had come from and... "Oh, dear," she said, looking closer at him. "That means—"

"Don't!" He held up his hand. "I don't want to talk about it."

"They're in here." The door opened and constables Marillo and Adams walked in, revolvers ready.

"No need for that," Mark snapped. "She's been subdued."

Marillo holstered his gun and nodded his head for Adams to check on Fiona. He walked up to Mark. "You must be the infamous Mark Spadina, from Toronto PD."

"In the flesh." Mark stood and held out his hand. Marillo took it reluctantly.

Marillo glanced at Charley. "We've got the details you provided the sergeant, but I'm going to need you to come down to the station to make a formal statement."

"Can it wait until later?" she asked. "I need to find my brother."

"Your brother's missing now?" Marillo asked. "I thought you said he'd gone to visit friends in Belleville?"

She shrugged. "It doesn't matter now."

"Of course, it does," Adams snapped. "You lied to us. Hampered our investigation."

"I didn't hamper anything. I knew he wasn't involved. And I was right."

"How long has he been missing?" At least Marillo sounded concerned. "Did you file a missing person report?"

"Not yet. He hasn't been gone that long," she lied. A missing person report would become public knowledge and she couldn't have that.

"Okay, well, try to make it to the station as soon as you can." Then he turned to Mark. "You, too, Spadina. There'll be more than a few questions about your involvement here."

"So, how do you propose we find Freddie," Mark asked once Marillo and Adams took Fiona away. "Did Miss MacDonald give you anything?"

"No, she didn't know about him. If she had, I'm sure she'd have told me."

"Then what's our next step? We've exhausted all our clues."

"We?" Charley asked.

"Of course, we."

"I assumed you'd be heading back to Toronto now you've discovered where Marjorie Dixon got her money and solved her murder. I think you have a lot of explaining to do to your superiors."

Mark shrugged. "They can wait. I'm not going to abandon you now."

Charley blinked away the tears welling up in her eyes. "Thank you."

"Besides, with your penchant for getting into a fix, you need me."

"Humph," she snorted, his comment successfully stemming the threatening tears. "We're not at a complete dead end yet."

When she saw the confused look on Mark's face she continued. "Marjorie Dixon would need to find a secluded place to take addicts. But we know she herself didn't have any money, so she couldn't purchase a property on her own."

"So, she'd have to get money from someone else," Mark said. "That would fit with what I learned about the other men she'd been involved with. Do you think your brother gave her money?"

"No, Gran cut him off when his drinking became a problem."

"But we haven't found any other—oh wait," Mark said. "The Cannons."

Charley nodded. "They claim they weren't being black-mailed, but..." She couldn't imagine they'd lie to her knowing Freddie's life was at stake, but she'd covered enough crime in the city to know self-preservation could bring up a person's baser instincts. "I need to call my researcher at the paper to see if she's turned up anything."

"I AM SO SORRY, Charley. Mother and I didn't know about the island, and my father didn't know about Freddie." Dan cast his eyes down. He couldn't stop apologizing.

Intrepid Grace had discovered a recent land transfer of a small island owned by the Cannons to a Toronto-based company.

Dan had been shocked when Charley had told him, but then confirmed with his father the sale had been made to a company at the request of Marjorie Dixon. Once the circumstances were explained, Ted couldn't have been more helpful, offering a speedboat and pilot capable of manoeuvring through the St. Lawrence River's Thousand Islands at night.

Charley glanced up at the setting sun. It was all taking so much longer than she wanted. She and Spadina had given their statements to the police. She'd hoped to postpone giving hers until after she'd found her brother, but Marillo had stationed an officer outside the lab who had, not so nicely, insisted they go with him.

"Here she comes," Dan said, pointing to the light that appeared rounding the curve to the shipyard. It approached at breakneck speed, but then the roaring engine cut out and the craft slowed, easing toward the dock. Dan glanced down at Charley, worry furrowing his brows. "Are you sure you want to come? You can wait here."

Charley swallowed past the lump in her throat. She could do this. "No, I need to go."

"It's not a problem if you want to wait here. We can handle this," Dan insisted.

"Why wouldn't she want to go?" Mark appeared beside her.

"Why are you still here?" Dan muttered.

"I've been with her from the start, Sport. From the first night she went looking for her brother in Portsmouth. Remember that night? The night you bailed on her and so she went alone?"

"What?" Dan whirled to face her.

"Enough!" Charley shifted her gaze between the two men—half-brothers—so different in many ways, but so very similar in others.

Pig-headed, the two of them.

"I will be fine." She squared her shoulders and raised her chin, determined not to show weakness.

"Is it seasickness? I can help with that."

Everyone turned toward the young female voice.

"You must be Laine Black," Charley said. Grace had suggested they bring a doctor with them in case Freddie needed immediate medical attention if—no, when!—they found him. Appreciating the need for discretion, she'd suggested her roommate, Laine, who was doing her residency in emergency medicine at Kingston General Hospital.

Charley introduced herself, and then Dan and Mark. She leaned against a pole on the dock, observing the doctor as she answered the men's numerous questions. Charley rolled her eyes. *Men.* They'd most likely never met a woman doctor before, let alone an attractive one.

Laine was petite, tiny even—she couldn't be much over five feet. Wisps of close-cropped dark hair peeked out from the multi-coloured scarf she'd tied around her head. The scarf was a striking contrast to the drab khaki jacket, dark pants and heavy black boots. She had a small pointed chin and pale blue eyes. Charley tried to imagine her commanding an emergency room but failed. Laine Black looked like an elf in military fatigues. The doctor broke away from the two men and approached Charley. "I can give you something for motion sickness," she said quietly.

"Thank you but no. It's not that."

Laine shrugged. "Okay. Let me know, though. Asking for help isn't a weakness, you know."

Charley watched as the boat nudged the dock. It wasn't as big as she'd expected—hoped for, really. It was wooden with a long nose and a low wooden cabin painted red and gold. About one-quarter of the boat's deck was open at the back.

Dan caught the rope tossed by the pilot and held the stern steady. "All aboard," he called.

Mark leapt onto the boat deck unaided. Laine handed Dan her large black bag and then accepted his hand for assistance before jumping down lithely.

"Last chance," Dan whispered as Charley approached.

"I'm going." She took his hand and climbed on board a boat for the first time in her life.

Only for you, Freddie. You better not be dead.

She stood immobile, uncertain where to go. Would it be safer inside the cabin? Or out here in the open?

Laine took her hand and led her to a bench in the centre of the cabin. "Less motion," she said.

Charley sat down and smiled weakly. Let them think she suffered from seasickness. Maybe that was better than revealing the truth. Dan knew, of course, but he wouldn't say anything.

"How long?" she asked the pilot.

"Forty minutes or so? She's pretty fast."

Forty minutes. She could do this.

The engine purred as the boat reversed away from the dock and turned toward the main channel. As the boat gained speed, the momentum pressed her back against the seat. Her fingers dug into the leather as she turned to watch the glowing lights of Kingston fade into the distance.

She couldn't remember how old she'd been when she equated the absence of her parents with their deaths. Gran and Grandpa never mentioned what had happened to them, and to this day, Gran refused to talk about it. But Frederick II and Cynthia Stormont had been prominent members of society, and their deaths had been widely reported. Charley had looked it up when she started working at the *Trib*. The headline would be forever emblazed in her memory: FREDERICK STORMONT AND WIFE DROWN IN BOATING ACCIDENT. Her parents, fervent and experienced sailors, had been returning from visiting friends in Cape Vincent, New York. Their bodies were found in the water, not far from where their sailboat had run aground. For days, the *Trib* had been full of tributes to the couple, but the reporting on the actual incident was sparse. New York State Police were baffled because the weather conditions had been ideal that day, but in the absence of any clear cause, it was eventually ruled an accident.

She jumped, startled, as Dan placed a bright orange life preserver around her neck.

He sat beside her, took her hand and squeezed it. "I've been trying to get you to go out in a boat with me for years. Trust Freddie to succeed where I've failed," he said with a wink.

She appreciated Dan trying to lighten her mood. Ironic —here she hated boats and yet her best friend was the scion of the area's pre-eminent shipbuilders and an Olympic-calibre rower. Dan loved being out on the water. It was a huge part of who he was—a part she couldn't share.

Finally, the motor quieted and Dan left to help the pilot secure the boat.

"You okay, Tiger?"

She glanced up. Mark's dark eyes held a flicker of worry. "Fine." She stood, stumbling slightly as the boat knocked against the dock. Mark caught her waist to steady her and she gave him a reassuring smile. "Let's go get Freddie."

"Have you been here before?" Charley asked Dan as they stood on the wooden dock gazing into the darkness of the island's interior.

"Years ago. My great-grandfather built a cottage here. I remember coming with my parents when I was quite young, but I don't think anyone's been here since my grandfather died, and that has to be twenty years or more." He swung one of the two lanterns he'd taken from the boat in a wide arc. "There used to be a small boathouse here, but with no one maintaining the property, it probably got demolished or swept away by the weather." He paused as a wolf bayed in the distance, and then glanced at Mark who held the second lantern. "You follow up the rear." He bent to pick up Laine's black bag, but she stopped him.

"Thanks, but I've got it."

They followed a trail leading from the end of the dock

through a growth of trees. "The island was pretty much stripped bare of its trees in the last century," Dan said as if he was giving a tour. Charley tried not to be irritated. She knew he was trying to keep her mind from going toward the worst-case scenario. "It's remarkable how quickly the forest has grown back."

She shivered as the wolf howled again.

"It looks like someone has done some work to clear the path," Laine said, giving Charley her first real ray of hope in days.

"Up there!" Charley pointed toward the two-storey, wooden structure peeking out from the trees. She rushed past Dan and climbed the steps of the front porch and pushed open the door. "Freddie!" she called into the darkness.

The lantern's light appeared behind her as Dan and Laine followed her into the cottage. It was a large, open room, sparsely furnished with a table and two chairs.

"Well, someone's been here," Laine said. "There's no dust or grime, not like you'd expect for a place that's been vacant for twenty years."

Charley walked to the kitchenette area. A portable stove rested on a countertop. "There are dishes in the sink." She spun around. "Freddie!"

"Upstairs?" Dan said, leading the way by taking two steps at a time. He threw open each of the three doors and shone his lantern into the rooms, but they were all empty.

Fear knotted Charley's gut as she considered all the terrible things that could have happened to her brother. Given her past mistakes, how could Marjorie Dixon have brought him to an island of all places? What if he'd fallen into the river, like Fiona's father? Or been attacked by a wolf?

"I was so sure—" Dan began.

"He has to be somewhere," Laine interrupted in the authoritative, no-nonsense tone of a physician. "We just need to keep looking."

As the three descended the stairs, it occurred to Charley that she hadn't seen Mark since she'd entered the cottage. She led the way onto the porch and spotted his light through the trees.

"Can you see anything?" she called.

"More than I want to," Mark called back. "You better get over here but be prepared. And for heaven's sake, someone please bring a blanket."

Mark stood in Charley's way, stopping her from advancing past him. "Go slow," he urged. "Take your time." Then he stepped aside and held up the lantern.

Ahead, now illuminated, Charley could see a human form, on hands and knees. Then the head reared back and let out a mournful howl.

Freddie?

"I realized if the island had been stripped of its trees, the wildlife would have been gone, too. So, while some animals may have been able to return, it is very unlikely a large predator, like a wolf, would have done so yet," Mark said, following closely behind her.

As she approached Freddie, her eyes widened, and she gasped in shock. Her brother was completely naked.

"I did warn you," he said. "Hallucinations at this stage aren't unusual."

"But they can be dangerous," Laine said, dropping her bag beside them. She rummaged inside, placed her stethoscope around her neck, and took out a syringe. "How heavy would you say he is?"

"What are you going to do with that?" Charley asked at the same time as Mark estimated, "Two-ten, maybe."

"If we are going to take him back, we are going to have to sedate him," Laine said.

"I can talk to him, calm him down. We don't have to drug him," Charley said.

"You can try," Laine said, not looking up from using the syringe to withdraw liquid from a small vial. "And then it's the phenobarbital."

"Here." Dan was panting as he handed her a blanket.

"Freddie," she said softly as she slowly approached her brother.

The glow of the lantern gave the dusting of red hair covering his body a golden sheen. He turned his head toward her, bared his teeth and growled.

She paused. "Freddie, it's me—Charley. I've come to take you home."

Still on all fours, he turned his body and moved toward her. His gaze locked with hers and she realized his eyes held no hint of recognition.

Closer he came. She could see sweat beading on his face despite the temperature hovering slightly above freezing. Her heart was beating furiously and, quite unbelievably, she felt afraid—not afraid *for* him, afraid *of* him. "Freddie," she whimpered. Her body tensed as she watched him rear back, preparing to launch himself at her.

And then he was pinned to the ground. Mark had his upper body and Dan his legs while Laine efficiently administered the barbiturate. Freddie thrashed against his captors for several minutes and then went quiet. Laine checked his heart and lungs with her stethoscope and gave a satisfied nod.

Charley knelt beside her brother and wrapped the

blanket around him. He was burning up. "Will he be all right?"

"I think so," Laine said. "I'll stay with him for the next twenty-four hours, but physically, the worst is over."

Charley stroked her brother's cheek, the soft bristles of his beard tickled her palm. She gently kissed his forehead. Physically, the worst may be over, but she knew Freddie had a long way to go before he would be healed.

For the first time in days, Charley could breathe. She glanced across the crowded room to her brother, perched on a chair as if he were a king on a throne, surrounded by the people who loved him most in the world. Family and friends had congregated to celebrate his thirty-second birthday. She caught his eye and he raised a glass of whiskey to salute her. She had to turn away.

Thirty-six hours ago, they'd found him naked and hallucinating from the effects of alcohol withdrawal and had brought him home to recover. Laine had stayed with him until the effects had worn off early this morning. It had been awful, but he'd survived, swearing he'd never touch alcohol again. Tonight, that promise, along with all the trials he'd endured the past five days, were forgotten. It broke her heart.

"He looks so happy, doesn't he?" Gran said, taking her arm for support. Charley feared she'd have a lot of explaining to do when they brought Freddie home unconscious, but it had been unnecessary. Apparently, her grandmother had been well aware Freddie had been missing for several days and was simply relieved to have him home— and in time for the party, as Charley had promised.

"I wish we weren't serving alcohol, Gran. It's too hard on Freddie."

"We can't possibly host a party without offering our guests something to drink," Gran chided her. "It's not prohibition, for heaven's sake. I'll tell the girl to get rid of it all tomorrow."

"He'll just go somewhere else," Charley said. "I've been looking into treatment programs. Maybe he can go to a hospital where they can—"

"I don't want to talk about any of that now. Freddie is home and he's safe. We will deal with everything else later. Oh, look, there's Mr. Sherman. I must go say hello."

Charley's gaze followed Bessie across the room where she welcomed the *Trib*'s managing editor.

Who invited him?

She sighed heavily. Her grandmother could be so modern, so forward-thinking on so many subjects. She had been a suffragette, after all. But there were still times when the traditionalism of her views and values surprised Charley. Gran, like so many of her contemporaries, believed Freddie's alcohol problems could be managed within the family. Charley didn't believe that anymore. He needed more help than they could give him.

"That's a pretty serious expression for a party," Mark said as he approached.

"I thought you'd be back in Toronto by now," she replied.

"You're always trying to get rid of me. Send me back to The Big Smoke. Maybe I like it here. Besides, I have yet to meet the mysterious Mr. Hall."

Charley closed her eyes and bowed her head. *Theo.* The other reason for her morose mood.

"I noticed there are two birthday cakes, one for your

brother and the other, I presume, is for your husband?" Mark looked around. "Is he here?"

"No." Her voice was barely a whisper. She squeezed her eyelids tighter, fighting the tears.

"I'm sorry." Mark dabbed her eyes with a handkerchief. "It's clean, I promise," he said after she'd opened her eyes and took it from him.

"I guess I do owe you an explanation," Charley said.

"You don't owe me anything," Mark said, looking uncomfortable.

"We both know that's not true," Charley said, doing her best to force a smile. "You've shared your secrets with me, it's only fair I do the same. Besides, it's not much of a secret. You're probably the only person here who doesn't know." She had a thought. "You're a detective. It wouldn't have taken much for you to learn about Theo. Why didn't you?"

Mark shrugged. "I figured it was your story to tell and you'd do so when—if—you wanted me to know."

She cocked her head to look up at him, surprised to see a warm glow of friendship in the eyes of this dark, menacing cop. He regularly surprised her.

"Freddie and Theo—Theodore Arthur Hall—my husband, were born on the same day. Our mothers were from England and had both married Canadian soldiers during the Great War. They met each other while on the ship travelling here, in 1917, and became good friends. Maybe it was because they each had a baby to take care of and that couldn't have been easy during an ocean crossing." Charley waved away Chantal who was approaching with a tray of *hors d'oeuvres*.

"The boys were inseparable, but they couldn't be more different," she continued. "Freddie was cautious and sensitive. Theo was, well, there's no other way to put it, he was a hellion. There was no challenge too great for him to take on. He protected Freddie, in many ways. He made sure the other boys didn't pick on him, as they often do with quieter, more studious boys."

She could picture them, two teenaged boys out to prove their stuff. She'd been three years younger and desperate to be included in their adventures. Freddie would try to shoo her away, but Theo would often allow her to tag along, taking on the burden of responsibility for her safety as well as her brother's. "Everyone loved Theo," she added.

"Including you," Mark said.

Charley sighed deeply, the pain of admission, of saying it out loud, almost too much. "Not as I should have." Mark's eyes widened. "Oh, don't get me wrong. I did love Theo. He was like a brother to me. When the war broke out, he convinced Freddie they should enlist. And he didn't want to go to war a bachelor. He said it would be better if he was married—give him someone to come home to. He and Freddie were all for the idea. Gran and Theo's parents, too. So, what could I do? I was twenty, should have been married already, according to Gran, and they were going *to war*. It seemed churlish to resist."

"So, you married him."

"We were married the first of December, and he and Freddie left for England ten days later."

"I'm assuming he didn't return."

Charley shook her head.

"I'm sorry."

"People tell me I should move on. Remarry. But I can't." She looked at Mark. This was the part no one understood. Not Dan. Not even Gran. "We don't know what happened to him. He was missing after Dieppe and..." her voice hitched, "...and we just don't know what happened. At first, we assumed he'd died. We thought the same of Freddie, too. For years, we heard nothing. Then, out of the blue, long after the war was over, we learned Freddie had survived in a POW camp. He came home to us."

"But no Theo."

She shook her head. "But he could still be out there. Don't you see? Freddie came home; maybe Theo will, too. And if—when—he does, I need to be waiting for him, as I promised."

There was pity in Mark's eyes as he gazed down at her. Pity and something else...

"You think I'm crazy?"

"No," he said. "I think you have moxie. You are probably the strongest, most selfless woman I have ever met." Then he grinned. "And a little crazy."

She snorted, relieved he'd broken the tension.

"So, tell me, if you hadn't married Theodore Arthur Hall, how did you see your life unfolding? Was there another beau you'd set your cap for?"

Without meaning to, her gaze travelled across the room to where Dan was chatting with several young women— granddaughters of Gran's book club friends. She tried not to be jealous.

Mark followed her gaze. "I see. Does he know?"

She shook her head. "Of course not. I am not free, and he has plans, a bright future ahead of him."

"Yadda, yadda, yadda," Mark said. "You're too good for him, anyway."

"Are you going to tell him?"

"About your infatuation with him?"

"No." Charley laughed. She knew her secret was safe with Mark. "Tell him the two of you are half-brothers."

"I think I'm going to let that sleeping dog lie for a time. I don't think either of us is ready for a family reunion."

"What are you going to do, then? Will you be heading back to Toronto soon?"

"There you go with trying to ship me off to Toronto again," he teased. "Actually, I'm not too popular with my superiors at the Toronto PD, right now. I thought I might stick around here for a while and give them some time to cool off."

"I'm glad," Charley said, and it surprised her to realize just how glad she was he'd be hanging around. Out of the corner of her eye, she spied John Sherman heading toward them. "Oh dear."

"Another beau?" Mark asked.

"Hardly. It's my boss from the *Trib*."

"Well, I'm going to grab another piece of cake. Chantal may not be able to scramble a decent egg, but she does make one heck of a chocolate cake."

After being in Mark's intense physical presence, Sherman seemed almost non-existent. His small stature made her feel gargantuan. "I wanted to tell you, you did an excellent job on the women's pages in today's edition," he said.

Charley was pleased with the profile she'd written about Fiona's life and struggles, and how it highlighted the vulnerability of women in society. She didn't know if it would make a difference in her defence, but at least her story had been told. And while it had been the main story on the front of the women's section, more important to Charley was the fact it was a carry-over from her article on the murder of Marjorie Dixon. That story had appeared, with her byline, above the fold on page one.

Take that Lester Pyne.

"Can I assume this means you'll accept my offer to take it over going forward?" he continued.

Charley gazed down at him. She could certainly subvert the women's pages for her own purpose, but if he thought it meant conceding her role as city reporter, too, he was in for a surprise. She extended her hand. "Mr. Sherman, you have a deal."

What's next for Charley?
When Dan Cannon is accused of murdering his old rowing nemesis, he asks Charley to prove his innocence. First, she learns the dead man was her father's best friend and rowing partner. Then the boat her parents had been sailing when they drowned twenty-give years ago mysteriously reappears swamping her in questions about her friend's connection to their deaths.

Find out whether Charley will sink or swim in *Rigged for Murder*. Keep reading for a sneak peek. Or scan the QR code to get it now.

Want more from Charley and her friends? Head over to my website and sign up for the *Gayle Gazette* to keep up-to-date on new releases, exclusive access to special features and giveaways. Plus, you'll get a free download of a solve-it-yourself *Bessie Stormont Whodunit*. Yup, Gran has some real detective skills, too. Scan the code to get your access.

HISTORICAL NOTES

While A *Shot of Murder* is fiction, there are some incidents in the story rooted in fact.

THE DEATH OF A PRISON GUARD

On April 26, 1948, Kingston Penitentiary guard and messenger John D. Kennedy, 58, was murdered during a violent escape by prisoners Austin Craft, 46, and Howard Urquhart, 21.

That morning Kennedy had picked up his car from the prison's garage and was driving across the compound to the North Gate. On the way, he was flagged down by Craft who was headed to the gate to meet the garbage truck, which was part of his prison job. Kennedy didn't realize that Urquhart, who worked in the prison's garage, was hiding in the trunk of his car. Once inside the gatehouse, Craft held Kennedy at gunpoint and demanded the keys to leave the penitentiary. Kennedy refused and was shot and killed. Craft then stole the keys, unlocked the main gate, and the pair sped away in the stolen vehicle.

Police across Ontario were notified, and a large-scale search of the area ensued. The men were found by two prison guards at around 1 p.m., hiding under some brush near the village of Sydenham, not far north of Kingston.

Urquhart was subsequently convicted of lesser charges for the prison break, but Craft was found guilty of Kennedy's murder and sentenced to death. His hanging, on January 24, 1949, was the last execution to occur in Kingston.

The information around Kennedy's birth, his home in Portsmouth and his funeral are also factual.

EYE COLOUR AND THE UNDERSTANDING OF GENETICS IN 1948

A key clue to solving the mystery of Marjorie Dixon's death comes from Fiona MacDonald when she reveals two blue-eyed parents could not produce a brown-eyed offspring. The theory that a single gene was responsible for eye colour, with the allele for brown eyes being dominant over blue, was developed by Charles and Gertrude Davenport in 1907, and taught to students for most of the twentieth century. We now know this is too simple an explanation and to date, at least eight genes have been identified as influencing eye colour. However, in 1948, the theory was unquestioned, no doubt leading to some erroneous assumptions about birthright.

SNEAK PEEK: RIGGED FOR MURDER

A CHARLEY HALL MYSTERY, BOOK 2

"Someone just filed a missing person on Alderman Cannon."

Charley Hall's head jerked up and she glared across the newsroom at the man who'd just made the pronouncement. It wasn't so much how the word "missing" landed like a punch to the gut that unnerved her as it was the glee in Lester Pyne's voice. He smelled a scoop.

"That's ridiculous," she said, rising from the desk she'd been relegated to. "I spoke to him not very long ago." In her head, she tried to figure out just when that had been. Surely it was only a day or two ago. He'd asked her to accompany him to a rowing regatta last weekend. When was that? Last Wednesday? Thursday, maybe? What day was today? Oh, heck. It was Wednesday, again. Had it really been a week? "Who would make such an outrageous claim?"

Pyne's pale face flushed, and he pounded his cigarette butt into the ashtray. The action knocked out several other discarded butts from the overfull bowl. "My contact says it was his secretary. A Miss Diana Huff."

Phew, Charley blew out her annoyance. What the heck was the woman thinking? Dan had probably simply forgotten to update her on his schedule and she, typically, was over-reacting.

"It's a legitimate lead," Pyne added defensively.

"What lead?" the *Kingston Tribune*'s managing editor, John Sherman, said from his doorway.

Shoot! Charley had hoped to nip Pyne's story before he ran with it, but now that Sherman was aware of it, she needed to find another solution. Even if Dan was missing—there was that word again—she needed to keep it out of the newspaper.

"Dan was in St. Catharines for a rowing regatta last weekend. He probably just took an extra day or two of vacation and forgot to let his secretary know," Charley said, crossing the room to stand beside her old desk. "If he was really missing, why wouldn't his parents have alerted the police?"

"Do we know if he made it to the regatta?" Sherman asked. Pyne shrugged and Sherman expelled an exasperated breath. "Well, find out."

Charley tried not to relish in the panic she saw on Pyne's face. She didn't dislike the man as much as resent him for taking her place as a city reporter. She appreciated he'd fought for his country—although, truth be told, she found it hard to envision the pudgy, baby-faced mama's boy in a military uniform—but did that mean she had to forfeit all she'd done to build her career as a top-notch reporter just so he'd have a job?

The world had changed while the men had been fighting Hitler and Tojo. Women had stepped up and proven themselves more than capable of making meaningful contributions to society. Surely there was a way for members of both sexes to work in harmony.

She knew Sherman's offer for her to take over the women's pages was meant to be an olive branch. And if it had been any other section of the newspaper, she would have viewed it as a promotion. But going from hard news to fashion and society reporting was a bitter pill to swallow. After all, she wasn't just an ordinary reporter. Her grandfather had founded the *Trib* half a century ago but was forced to sell it during the economically turbulent 1930s. Still, the Stormont name was held in high regard by the new publisher—indeed, by everyone in the news business.

After two months, Charley still wasn't completely comfortable with her new role. Although she was doing the work, she'd refused to have her name listed as editor on the masthead, and she balked when Sherman had proposed she use her maiden name, Charlotte Stormont. Along with articles about the latest fashions or who had attended what fundraiser, she had managed to slip in stories of more consequence, such as the plight of war widows or destitute mothers. So far, no reader had complained, so Sherman had turned a blind eye.

Nevertheless, she was determined to get her old job back. Pyne wasn't up to the challenge. Sherman would eventually have to acknowledge that. She glanced at her editor, but he wasn't looking at his city reporter for answers. He was staring at her.

Fine! She'd step in and rescue Pyne—again. *Kindness not knives, kindness not knives.* She repeated the mantra her grandmother had drilled into her since childhood.

"Martin?" she called to the sports editor whose desk was even farther removed than her own from the action of the newsroom. "Did you cover the rowing regatta in St. Catharines over the weekend?"

"Jeez, Charley," Stan Martin said, ambling over to the group, "I thought you read the *Trib* cover-to-cover."

It was a running joke between Charley and Stan that she never read the sports pages and he never read the rest of the paper. Stan had been a mentor to her since she'd first started out as a copy editor, and he'd been almost as incensed as she was over her removal from the city beat.

"Humour me," she replied.

"There was a two-page spread in Monday's edition. The regatta was a big deal because it determined who will represent Canada in rowing at the Olympics next month."

"Did Dan Cannon compete?"

"Sure did. Single sculls. Won his class quite handily, too."

Charley was pleased for Dan. He'd been a lifelong member of the Frontenac Rowing Club and had captained the Queen's University team almost a decade ago. Recently, he'd turned his focus toward the London Olympics as a way to raise his profile before entering federal politics.

She turned back to Sherman. "So, we know where he was this past weekend. I don't think there's a story here."

"There's an official missing person report." Pyne ran his hand over his head, nervously combing the thinning blond strands of hair. "The police are involved."

"Are you sure your source isn't mistaken?" Charley asked, wondering who on the force was feeding Pyne information.

"He's rock solid."

"So, we've got a missing person report filed by Cannon's secretary and police verification," Sherman said. "That's good enough for me. Let's run with it."

"Wait!" Charley glared at the two men. "You can't mention the cop unless you want Pyne's source to dry up. And as for the missing person report, I am not sure Diana Huff is all that reliable. All you're going to be able to write is 'anonymous sources claim a city alderman has gone missing.' That's not good journalism."

"What do you suggest, then?" Pyne's pasty white face turned pink.

Charley turned to Sherman. "I know the family. Let me talk to Dan's parents, see if there's any truth to this." She glanced back at Pyne before continuing. "You know the stature of the Cannons in this city. We don't want to write any half-baked stories that haven't been corroborated."

"You've got a point." Sherman pushed his round spectacles up onto his head and rubbed his eyes.

"But it's my story." Realizing his scoop was about to slip through his hands, Pyne's voice had risen an octave.

"It's not a story at all until it's been substantiated, and Hall is in the best position to do that," Sherman said.

"Think of the reputation of the *Trib*," Charley said, unable to stop the dig. She'd given away several of her own scoops to Pyne in the best interest of the paper. "We're all on the same team, right?"

Pyne sank into his chair, deflated. "I guess so."

"And if you want to give me the name of your contact at Kingston PD..." Charley gave him a saccharine smile. She knew he wouldn't, but she wanted him to refuse in front of their boss.

Sorry, Gran. Sometimes a sharp edge is required.

"Can't do that. I promised him anonymity."

"You confirm the tip, Hall," Sherman said, turning back toward his office. "I'll expect ten inches by deadline."

Want to read more? Scan the QR code to get *Rigged for Murder*, book 2 in the Charley Hall Mystery series.

ACKNOWLEDGEMENTS

Writing is a solitary pursuit but publishing a book is not. I am forever grateful to two talented author/editors who are instrumental in bringing my stories to you.

Joanna D'Angelo, my friend and editor, who suggested I write a mystery series and brainstormed ideas with me during a long drive to Toronto and back—and then hounded me until I actually wrote it.

Carolyn Heald, a historian, archivist and talented writer in her own right, she is also—and truly fortunate for me—an excellent copy editor who is very familiar with the city of Kingston as well as proper grammar.

In addition, over the past year I have been supported by the great team at Best Page Forward, who have taught me so much about the self-publishing world.

Finally, I want to express my sincere appreciation to the members of the Ottawa Romance Writers, the Women's Fiction Writers Association, Crime Writers of Canada, and Sisters in Crime, who provide unconditional support and a safe space to ask questions in this strange world of fiction writing.

ABOUT BRENDA GAYLE

I've been a writer all my life but returned to my love of fiction after more than 20 years in the world of corporate communications—although some might argue there is plenty of opportunity for fiction-writing there, too. I have a Master's degree in journalism and an undergraduate degree in psychology. A fan of many genres, I find it hard to stay within the publishing industry's prescribed boxes. Whether it's historical mystery, romantic suspense, or women's fiction, my greatest joy is creating deeply emotional books with memorable characters and compelling stories.

Connect with me on my website at BrendaGayle.com & sign up for *The Gayle Gazette,* my newsletter, to keep up-to-date on new releases, exclusive access to special features, giveaways, and all sorts of shenanigans. And don't forget, as a subscriber, you'll get a free download of a *Bessie Stormont Whodunit.*

Until next time...

ALSO BY BRENDA GAYLE

CHARLEY HALL MYSTERY SERIES

A Shot of Murder

Rigged for Murder

A Diagnosis of Murder

Odds on Murder

Murder in Abstract

Schooled in Murder

Made in United States
Troutdale, OR
12/28/2023

16485742R20116